Other titles by

KATRINA BRITT
IN HARLEQUIN ROMANCES

KATRINA BRITT

girl in blue

Harlequin Books

TORONTO • LONDON • NEW YORK • AMSTERDAM • SYDNEY

Harlequin Presents edition published October 1977
ISBN 0-373-70707-X

Original hardcover edition published in 1976
by Mills & Boon Limited

CHAPTER ONE

FELICITY Vale-Norton was said by her friends to be a very sweet and thoroughly nice young woman, kind, thoughtful, generous and much sought-after by most eligible males. That she was twenty-five and still unmarried was often a matter of comment, since she was very pretty, extremely feminine and liked men. Small-boned, exquisitely made with deep blue eyes and golden hair, she had the fragile kind of looks most appealing to men.

She was popular with both sexes and her gift for friendship ensured her a full social life; it was a good life and, at the moment, she wanted no other. Her days were full, and passed far too quickly for her to pause and wonder where she was heading until the day after her twenty-fifth birthday.

She opened her eyes sleepily, looked around the familiar charming bedroom with its bronze velvet curtains flowing elegantly from tall windows on to the cream carpet, and realized that she was now twenty-five.

Living in the country remote from the pressures of everyday life as she did, it was easy to drift along on a sea of enchantment surrounded by the beauties of nature.

Norton Towers, the home of the Vale-Nortons for centuries, was set in unspoiled countryside, where a sparkling stream meandered in wooded valleys forming acres of sweet serenity. Felicity loved her home with a deep devotion; loved the spacious, immaculate grounds from the ornate double gates at the beginning of the long tree-shaded drive to the massive pile of mellowed stone with its tall, mullioned windows often turned to flame in the setting sun.

Early morning meant a canter on Sandy, with her hair streaming in the breeze and her heart beating in tune to

Sandy's hooves on the soft jumble of fern and grass. Sometimes she was joined by her father, and by her twin brother Blain when he was on leave from his regiment.

Felicity was on excellent terms with her parents and she was well aware of being the apple of her father's eye. In her eyes, Colonel Vale-Norton was lovely, dignified and tweedy and perfectly cast in his role of a country gentleman, while Elvira Norton lived only for her son Blain.

Blain was a captain in the Guards, handsome and audacious, with an eye for the girls. He had his full share of the Vale-Norton charm and Felicity adored him; they had frolicked through every birthday together, and the one the previous evening had been as successful as the rest.

Felicity had floated lightly through every dance, and had had a number of proposals which she modestly put down to the amount of champagne in which her partners had indulged.

Wonderful party, wonderful everything! It was only now, when Anna came to draw back the velvet curtains and let in the clear, cool morning air, that cold reason returned. For no reason at all a shiver ran down Felicity's spine: it seemed to her in that unguarded moment that she was riding blindly along and that sooner or later she would meet catastrophe.

Usually at eight o'clock every morning Anna pulled back the curtains, gave Felicity an appetising breakfast tray and wished her good morning, but this morning it was ten because of the party the previous evening. But Felicity's smile had all the usual warmth, and she began to talk about the birthday party, since Anna knew practically everyone there.

Anna listened and made the usual comments, with a meaning glance at Felicity's ringless left hand when the male guests were mentioned. Felicity's way of fighting shy of any entanglements caused her concern when she looked back on her own uneventful spinsterhood, which was none

6

Felicity's soft lips had tightened. 'So does she, you idiot—she has nothing to lose. You have everything.'

With this parting shot she had stalked from the room, leaving him helping himself to another drink when normally she would have persuaded him to leave it and go to bed.

'I wish Blain could find a nice girl,' she said to Anna who had straightened the room and was on her way to the door.

'Well, at least he can't have a baby,' was that lady's comment as she left the room.

Staring at the closed door, Felicity was aware that Blain was full of the *joie de vivre* of which she knew very little. Her sheltered life at the Norton Towers had given her a very limited opportunity for discrimination or selection where men were concerned. She was as yet too inexperienced to fully understand her own character, much less that of her brother. All of which gave her food for thought.

Felicity was essentially her father's girl. Like him she was a bit of a dreamer and an idealist, and so far nothing had happened to challenge these two qualities. She had a healthy contempt for shallow people who had no depth of character, but to her Blain's weakness for drink and women was only his extreme youth clamouring for expression. She knew he was sound enough in character underneath.

To her great surprise and pleasure, Blain joined her when she went for a ride on Sandy. Anger never lasted long with Blain; he was his usual charming self. That afternoon he took her to the races. Her father went too, and Felicity thought he looked a poppet in his grey top-hat and his immaculate suit with the buttonhole. His old-world charm, his air of simple dignity, made him an arresting figure and she was very proud of him.

She hoped Blain would grow out of his dissolute ways and model himself upon his father, then she felt a little guilty at sitting on judgement on Blain since he endeavoured to take every care of her, giving her lunch and setting himself out to amuse her. He was so successful that when they went for afternoon coffee beneath the shade of trees at gay umbrella-topped tables, Felicity was her happy self.

Lounging in his chair, with his grey topper set rakishly on his fair curls, he smiled at her over the top of his racing card.

'You've brought me luck,' he said. 'I'm taking you out to a show tonight and supper afterwards.'

Felicity, bearing in mind the innumerable cheques she had slipped him out of her allowance to help him out of embarrassing situations, said anxiously, 'Sure you can afford it?'

'I wouldn't ask you if I couldn't,' he replied, adding with a wide grin, 'and I shan't be asking for a loan either.'

Felicity looked at him gravely as he lounged in his chair with the grace of luxurious ease and she noticed again the perfection of his features. His well-shaped head, his neat ears, his clear-cut profile, the squareness of his forehead and that chin with the dimple in the centre. His eyes, a lighter blue than her own, and his rather sensuous mouth.

'I'll remind you of that later,' she told him.

The show they went to see that evening was good and they went to supper afterwards as Blain had promised. More than one pair of eyes followed the slim, girlish figure and her handsome escort as they threaded their way through the tables in the rather exclusive restaurant which Blain had chosen. They had almost reached their table when a beautifully manicured white hand descended on Blain's immaculate arm and the owner leaned forward to speak to him.

'Hello, Blain,' said Nora Staffordly. 'How did you enjoy the show? We were several rows behind you.'

She was in the company of two men and another woman. She was beautifully dressed, with stones glittering at her throat and in her ears. A *femme fatale*, Felicity thought, who wore her beauty like a banner.

Blain extricated himself from a rather awkward situation with admirable aplomb.

Gallantly, he said, 'We enjoyed it immensely. And you?'

The lovely eyes moved from his boyish grin to Felicity, who gave a polite smile.

'We enjoyed it too. Won't you join us?' she replied after a pause.

'Sorry. This is my treat to Felicity.' Blain gave a click of the heels and a salute. 'Thanks. Some other time.'

They had settled at their table and Blain had given his order to the wine waiter, when Felicity looked at him with twinkling blue eyes.

'You did that rather well,' she admitted with a chuckle. 'I see what you're up against. She's certainly very lovely.'

Blain, decidedly red about the ears, said sheepishly, 'She's a very good dancer.'

Rather dryly, she spoke without rancour. 'Would you say she was a good all-round performer?'

Blain went scarlet. 'Here, hold on,' he protested, and she had to laugh.

'I was only teasing. You really are like a little boy sometimes, I don't know whether to spank you or kiss you.' She shook her head. 'I wish you would be more discreet.'

The wine had arrived and he poured it, handing her a glass gravely.

'I'm not with you,' he said perversely.

'You don't want to be, do you, Blain? You're like an ostrich who digs his face in the sand.' Felicity's voice was quiet and tinged with sadness. 'I've always been so proud of Daddy because he's a man of integrity—'

The well kept hand holding his drink trembled a little. 'And I'm not. Is that what you're trying to say?'

He raised his head and his eyes glittered. To Felicity his bearing was both bold and pathetic in that poignant capacity he had for heartbreak and defiance in one breath. She wanted to reach out and stroke his flushed cheek and

11

squeeze his hand.

Soothingly, she said, 'You're too young to form any real character yet. Neither of us have proved ourselves.' She raised her glass. 'Here's to us. May we never let the parents down.'

They drank and she looked at him from under her lashes as the meal progressed. It was so wonderful to have someone who was part of herself. If only he was more dependable! But there was nothing she could do but love him for what he was.

Two days later Blain left his family, saying that he had promised to spend the rest of his leave with a friend in London.

'Take care,' said Felicity when she kissed him goodbye. 'Find a nice girl.'

Blain hesitated for a moment. Then he kissed her soundly and said in his soft caressing way, 'I'm too young to marry, but I promise to be a good boy.'

Elvira Vale-Norton was always in an awkward mood whenever her son went back to his regiment. At these times, Felicity felt sympathy and frustration bubbling up inside her as it constantly occurred to her that her mother's indulgence of her male offspring was largely responsible for Blain's weakness of character. She had never allowed him to stand up to the results of his own irresponsibilities.

A few days after he had gone Felicity entered the lounge, with its tall windows overlooking the lovely sweep of the green countryside, to find her mother seated at her writing desk. She was making out cheques which Felicity was sure were for Blain's debts. Despair seized her by the throat as she saw the act as one encouraging Blain's extravagant tastes.

With her eyes on her mother's slim, straight back, she walked across the deep pile carpet.

'Mother,' she said, 'do you ever pause to think whether

you're being fair to Blain in settling his debts so readily? He has to grow up some day and learn to accept responsibility. Some day he'll marry, and you're not being fair either to him or the girl who will eventually be his wife.'

Elvira continued with her task, putting the cheques and bills in their envelopes and sealing them down leisurely. Then, pushing back her chair, she turned to look up at her daughter's worried face. Her smile had a singular and compelling charm.

'Blain is only sowing his wild oats,' she told her gently. 'I give him a helping hand. Why shouldn't he live for the moment with the world as it is today forever hovering in the brink of disaster? Anything can happen.'

'Exactly,' Felicity replied. 'How can he face up to hard knocks if you insist on wrapping him in cotton wool?'

Elvira shook her head. 'You're jealous of him. We'll say no more about it.'

Felicity clenched her hands. 'Jealous?' she echoed. 'If that were true, I would say nothing and let you send him to the devil. I love Blain as much as you do, maybe more, for I could never deliberately ruin him as you're doing.' Her winged brows drew together in a look of distress. 'I also have to stand by and watch you slowly destroy him, watch you ruin his chances of ever becoming anything worth while. All his life he's taken what he wants regardless of other people's feelings. He has a surfeit of everything he likes, he'll begin to take more and more.'

She walked over to one of the windows to gaze out unseeingly, with blurred vision. When she went on her voice was husky with emotion.

'I'm frightened for him, frightened at what women like Nora Staffordly can do to him, frightened for his future. He won't listen to me. Why should he, when you're there to give him everything he wants?'

In the silence which followed Elvira walked across the room to where Felicity stood silhouetted against the win-

13

dow and slipped an arm around her slender quivering form.

'My dear,' she said softly, 'don't you think I worry about him too? I saw my folly too late, but if I hadn't helped him with his debts he would have been cashiered long ago. Unfortunately, he was born with a fondness for luxuries and I've given them to him. Easy come, easy go. They could bore him in time, and then he'll come home to his mother.'

Felicity whirled out of her mother's arm and stared at her in exasperation.

'You don't want him to get married, do you? You want him to be with you, like the little boy who never grew up.'

'You, Felicity,' said her mother, 'are hysterical.'

'Thanks,' Felicity said shortly.

To Felicity's sensitive spirit her mother's indifference to herself was nothing to the realization that in indulging in her son's demands she had taken something infinitely precious—something he so badly needed, and which a mother alone could give him. Her distress went deeper, because she felt as guilty herself as she had accused her mother of being. Blain had been a dominant motive in her own life, her complete devotion to him and all his interests something which made itself part of her life, of the air she breathed.

The soft closing of the door told her that her mother had left the room. Her first impulse was to go after her, to quiet her apprehensions that she would break in again on that temple of hers. But Felicity knew that her mother had never understood her nor made any attempt to do so. With a deep sigh she opened the French window and stepped out into the sunlight, wishing she could see beyond the grounds into the distant future hidden from her by the mists of time. Pushing her hands into the pockets of her linen dress, she strolled through the grounds, her cheeks flushed as they often were when coming into contact with her mother. She was only too accustomed to her indifference. She spoke a different language but, in her own concern for Blain's future, she had hoped for once that she could touch some chord for herself that her mother kept hidden. Now she was desperately hurt because there was none there, and a little bitter.

'I'm a fool to care,' she said fiercely to herself, and with that she walked determinedly away from the house.

That evening Felicity had a telephone call from Blain. His voice sounded thick and strange.

'Felicity?' he queried, and at the sound of her voice he continued, 'I have to see you as soon as possible. How soon can you come up to Town?'

'Tomorrow morning, if it's urgent.'

'Good. I'm in a devil of a mess,' he said urgently. 'Don't tell the parents you're coming to see me.'

'Very well,' she agreed. 'I'll see you in the usual place at half-past twelve. You're at the barracks?'

'Yes. My leave was up last night. Don't let me down, will you?'

'Have I ever? I'll be there.'

She put the phone down on a shiver of premonition, wondering what he had been up to this time. It could not be money troubles since all his debts had been settled. Something far worse, probably, she thought, and trembled. Sooner or later he was going to go too far.

She drove up to London the following morning and parked the car. The sun had brought out the usual crowds as she made her way to the restaurant where they usually met when she was in Town. Blain was there wearing his dress uniform, dark blue with red stripes, and the uniform becked hat set rakishly on his fair curls.

He was the target for all feminine eyes, and Felicity wished desperately that he was tubby with a squint as he grinned down at her.

'Thanks for coming,' he said. 'I knew I could rely on you.'

'That's been the trouble,' she began as he took her arm and they went inside the restaurant. 'Maybe you'll have to fight this one out yourself.'

But Blain was not listening. With his usual charm he was being led to one of the best tables near a window, secluded but with a view of the room, by a waiter who was already under his spell.

Felicity studied him from beneath her eyelashes as they sat down in an uneasy silence, broken at last by Blain's order to the waiter. Whatever his trouble was, she was sure he wouldn't learn a lesson from it.

'I've been a fool,' he admitted with self-abnegation, attacking his hors d'oeuvres as if it was responsible.

Hardening, Felicity murmured, 'I shall put that down as the understatement of the year. What's new?'

The tips of his ears reddened and he looked sheepish. 'You're going to despise me for going back on my word to you. The truth is, I cut my leave short to go away with Nora Staffordly to Paris.'

A chill feathered down her spine. 'Go on,' she said.

He moistened dry lips. 'It was sheer bad luck that her husband happened to book in at the same hotel. He spends most of his time abroad on business, and Nora understood he was in Italy.'

Felicity nearly choked on a portion of food. 'Blain, you fool! After all I said!' Anger at his stupidity made her voice scathing. 'I suppose he caught you with her, or did you book in under assumed names?'

He gulped down part of his wine as if to give him courage. 'One of the maids who knew Nora came to our room to tell us, so I packed and left.' He put down the glass with a shaky hand. 'But he knew I'd been there with her. Nora rang me up to tell me.'

'I see. And what's he going to do now?'

'He's threatened to divorce her and name me as co-respondent,' he said heavily.

16

'Charming,' Felicity said grimly. 'What are you going to do about it?'

Blain shrugged philosophically. 'Wait and see. He could change his mind. I'm due to go on manoeuvres next weekend for a month, then I shall take a course on service overseas. I could go abroad, if the worst comes to the worst, until it all blows over.'

'Just like that. What about the parents? You know how proud Daddy is of his good name, and Mummy will be distracted.'

Felicity's face was pale now. She was angry and unhappy, but at the same time she was sorry because he was not entirely to blame.

He lifted miserable eyes. 'It's Dad who bothers me. I can manage Mother.'

'Can you? Pity you can't manage your own affairs better.'

Felicity put down her knife and fork, having lost her appetite. For the first time in her life she was seeing her illusions swept away, seeing her life at Norton Towers as something restricted and unreal. She swallowed painfully, and Blain saw the tears in her eyes with a sense of shame.

Yet he felt quite magnanimous when he said, 'I'm sorry, old girl, I know you must think me a first-rate cad. Of course I don't expect you to understand. After all, I'm a man.'

Her eyes were clear now of tears. She looked directly at him.

'Are you?' she asked meaningly.

He did not answer. He did not quite understand what she meant, and thought it politic to remain silent.

'Why did you do it?' she insisted.

Blain reddened and endeavoured to explain.

He said, 'When a woman is easy game no man is likely to throw the chance over his shoulder. You see what I mean?'

She nodded. 'I can also see that you've never understood

what I mean. That's the tragic part of it. You and I might be twins, but we have a far different set of values. Everything in life has been yours for the taking. Up to a point it's been mine too, only a woman is not like a man. She can't have her cake and eat it without becoming a tart in the process. I love you very much, Blain,' her smile was poignantly tender, 'I always will. That's another funny thing about women. Their capacity for loving and compassion far exceeds that of men. Looks as if we have a fight on our hands!'

It took him several seconds to digest her meaning. Then he gave a laugh of pure relief.

'You mean you'll stand by me?'

She nodded. 'That's what sisters are for.'

CHAPTER TWO

FELICITY was a few days recovering from Blain's news, and his regiment had gone on manoeuvres when she finally settled down into the old routine. Her life reverted again to its pristine freshness and she kept lots of engagements in between giving dinner parties for her friends. Everything was fun again and extremely pleasant. Not that she did not miss Blain; she did, enormously, for he coloured her life and she thought of him often.

Thinking of him set her off examining her own way of life and her beliefs—that tendency to expect from others what she had no right to expect. Blain was only human, and a member of the permissive present-day society from which she had kept herself more or less separate.

She longed to discuss Blain's affair with Nora Staffordly, but decided this was one thing she could not mention to anyone, not even the admirable Anna. She had lain awake at night seeking some way of communicating with her father on the subject of Blain. He was the one she always went to for advice, but Blain was the one person she could not discuss with him. It was really amazing to her how different a son could be from his own father.

The Colonel was no fool. He must have been increasingly conscious that his son was drinking too much. Maybe he was not unduly concerned because Blain's excellent health was not yet impaired.

Some time, Felicity promised herself, she would approach the subject of Blain in a casual way to her father and endeavour to bring him nearer to his son. Colonel Vale-Norton was as cynical as any man of his age and experience on the frailty of the human race, but he loved his children, she was sure of that.

As she cast around for someone to confide in, Anna supplied a clue.

'David Colston rang three times yesterday while you were out. He's back again from his diggings. Thought you'd like to know,' she said on a casual note as she drew back the curtains in Felicity's bedroom.

Felicity took the top off her egg with slender, well-cared-for hands. David Colston was one of the few men she had learned to trust. He was a bachelor of twenty-eight and well-to-do, but he also had a domineering mother. And he played golf, which Felicity did not.

He was not too good-looking, but he dressed well and only dined in the most exclusive places. His mother was a close friend of Elvira's and they very often got together, talking about the merits of their boys. Felicity had seen too much of what a mother's killing devotion could do to a son via Blain, and she did not fancy a Blain for a husband. Nevertheless, she had gone out with David quite often before he had gone away on an archaeological venture abroad with friends.

Unlike Blain, David had been more interested in swinging a golf club than a pretty woman, and Felicity had been rather surprised when he had asked her for a date one evening at a dinner party. She soon discovered that he did not have much in common with her own circle of friends, yet she went on seeing him because he amused her in a lazy, nonchalant kind of way.

The final disillusion had come when she had gone to see him play in a golf tournament. He had been winning, until the last two holes, which were his undoing. He was a terrible loser and what she regarded as a poor sport. After that, she spaced out her dates with him, which only served to make him more eager. He began to telephone her at all hours, and there had been something missing from the day when Anna did not say, 'He rang again,' he being David.

Since learning of Blain's disturbing affair with Nora

Staffordly, Felicity had resolved to alter her own life from its serene peaceful existence to a more revealing one. It had also occurred to her that if she was to make a good marriage, Blain would take note and follow suit.

'Did he leave any message?' she asked, scooping out a spoonful of golden yolk from her egg.

'He's calling today after lunch,' Anna said. 'I can tell him you're out.'

'I'll be in. He's not so bad when he's tanned,' Felicity murmured dreamily over her egg.

When he arrived just after lunch, he looked tanned but harassed.

'Felicity darling,' he cried, taking her hands into his hard calloused ones, 'I've missed you like hell. You have to marry me.'

To say that she was taken aback was to put it mildly.

'But why?' she asked, staring at him as if he had taken leave of his senses.

'For the obvious reasons. You're bright, chic, beautiful and everything a man could look for in a wife. And I love you.'

Still reeling from the shock, Felicity said the first thing that came into her head.

'But I don't love your mother.'

'What has she to do with it?' He ran his hand through his hair, a trick of his when he was losing at golf, and she was sure he was not going to be a good loser in the marriage stakes either. 'You won't be marrying my mother.'

'I shall if I marry you,' she told him.

'You mean you won't marry me?'

He looked as put out as if he had just lost a golf tournament, and she nodded, feeling sorry for him.

Softening the blow, she said, 'I like you a lot, but marriage is so final. At least it is for me.'

'My arm doesn't exactly ache from notching up my divorces either. I've never proposed to a girl before,' he said

21

sarcastically.

Felicity blushed and tried to look demure. 'I'm sure you haven't.'

'Sure you know what you're doing?' he asked darkly.

'Yes.' She nodded, wondering if she had been too hasty. David was not a bad sort, but that was not exactly a good reason for marrying him. A pity, she would miss him, and the thought of Blain being away too made her feel rather deflated.

David did not stay for tea. He left, still advising her to think it over; she was sure it had never occurred to him that she would decline the honour he had done her in asking her to be his wife. Maybe she was a little mad, for she suddenly ached to feel a strong arm around her other than her father's. Perhaps if David had slid an arm around her tenderly, she might have forgotten he had a mother and accepted him. The trouble was, she had turned down so many proposals that it could be becoming a habit. And all this heartsearching because of Blain! She was happy enough before.

Blain returned unexpectedly one evening. Her parents had gone out to dine with friends, and he was there in the lounge when she went down to dinner. He was in his favourite position, lounging in a chair with one leg slung over the arm, and he looked shattered. Immediately on seeing his face, Felicity knew the worst had happened.

He had a drink in his hand and, as she entered, he threw a long official-looking envelope on to the low table between them.

'I received this when I returned from manoeuvres this morning—notice of pending divorce proceedings from Staffordly. I came as soon as I could. He's naming me as co-respondent,' he said heavily.

He ran his hand through his curly hair, filled with an acute sense of resentment and self-pity before dashing off the remainder of his drink.

Felicity was divided between wanting to comfort him and telling him to take his punishment like a man. Instead, she said gently, 'You'll have to tell Daddy.'

'I know. What am I to do? He'll go berserk.'

'I don't think he will. You've come at the right time. He and Mummy are dining out and he'll come home replete with a good meal, which will put him in a favourable mood,' Felicity assured him practically. 'You're just in time for dinner.'

'If it wasn't for the sordidness of the whole affair, I would be glad this has happened,' said the Colonel, who on his return home had been greeted with the buff-coloured message from his erring son. 'It gives you the opportunity to be a man, and to grow up out of that cocoon of cotton wool your mother has wrapped you in all these years.'

He folded the document, having taken the news with admirable calm. Then he looked hard at his son, who reminded him of his own youth—there was the same familiar look of pride in the set of his head, the same soldierly bearing and tilt of the chin. There the resemblance ended. Felicity's face was warmer, more full of character. Her deep blue eyes beneath the lovely tilted brows were eloquent with feeling, her mouth tender and as charmingly expressive as her slender hands. Blain, he decided ruefully, had been pipped at the post by his twin when characters had been handed out. They were the wrong way round.

Blain, fortified by an excellent dinner and more than one double whisky, had stood the ordeal very well. He had the grace to look ashamed.

'I'm sorry, sir,' he said respectfully. 'I'm afraid the publicity won't do me any good as regards a future career in politics, as you'd planned for me.'

The Colonel stood up and threw the letter on the heavy mahogany table, then walked to the telephone.

'Pity you didn't think of that before,' he said grimly. 'I must get in touch with Callow right away.'

When the Colonel had left the room, Elvira went up to her son and put her arms around him protectively.

'Darling boy,' she cooed, 'don't worry. We shall get you out of this mess. The important thing is that you're home again. I have missed you, my pet.'

Felicity, raising her eyes to heaven, left the room quietly, leaving them together. She wished she could feel as optimistic about the affair as her mother. Blain, of course, would revel in his mother's petting.

Edward Callow, the family solicitor, came to dinner the following evening. He had been too busy to call earlier. He was a tall, ascetic-looking man who gave the impression that he had not been surprised at anything in his long career. In his late fifties, he was quick in his movements and eagle-eyed.

Over dinner, he said, 'I shall have to contact Staffordly's solicitor to see if there's any likelihood of the case being settled out of court. The divorce would have to go through the usual channels, but there is just a chance that it can be settled amicably, keeping Blain's name out of it. I won't promise anything.'

'In that case,' said the Colonel, plying him with more wine as though to keep him in a tolerable frame of mind, 'I shall contact Curtis Moreau, and ask him to take the case.'

Edward Callow shook his head. 'I'm afraid Moreau is above taking a case like this, but I don't say that it might not be possible to persuade him, seeing that he's an old ... er ... hmm ...' He cleared his throat, mindful of his profession and the danger of the spoken word. 'I believe he is an old acquaintance of Mrs Staffordly.'

'Who isn't?' thought Felicity scathingly.

After several attempts to contact Curtis Moreau by telephone, the Colonel sent him an invitation to spend the weekend at Norton Towers. He accepted. Norton Towers was the ideal place for any kind of discussion over good wine and expensive cigars; the original character of the

24

rooms had been preserved despite the modern decor. The beautiful panelling, the graciously carved antique pieces blended happily with the sophisticated modern decor with every bedroom having a small lounge and bathroom adjoining. There was also a billiard room.

Curtis Moreau was driving down on Friday night, and Felicity awaited his coming wishing it was all over. He would spoil a pleasant weekend, since Blain was coming too. While she dressed for dinner that evening, she tried to remember what she had heard about the famous Q.C. She recalled that he was both brilliant and young, about thirty, that he was one of the most successful and feared men at the bar. There was a faint recollection of having seen his streamlined form several times in one of the glossy magazines, photographed at some important function or other, but she had always regarded photographs as being misleading and she had never studied him. Now she was wishing she had.

Rather unfairly, Felicity was blaming him entirely for spoiling her weekend. She hated the thought of not being able to do what she liked, and wondered fleetingly if marriage was for her after all.

'I'm not in the mood for visitors, Anna,' she said as the woman came to see if she needed any help in dressing when she had helped Elvira. 'I'd like to stay in my room tonight and play records.'

She gave a little grimace as Anna's deft fingers piled her golden hair on the top of her head in curls.

'I've never known you to be scared of a man before,' observed Anna.

Felicity stiffened with indignation. 'Scared? What are you talking about?' Her clear blue eyes met those of her companion in the mirror.

Anna shrugged. 'Everyone knows that Curtis Moreau is the most eligible man about town. Every mother in *Who's Who* is panting after him for her daughter.' She gave a final pat to her handiwork and stepped back to survey the result. 'He'll make a nice change, a new face. You need a wider choice for a husband.'

'And who said I was looking for a husband?' Felicity demanded crossly.

'If you aren't, then it's time you were. I never knew anyone more in need of a husband.'

'Thanks! I never knew I looked so sex-starved. Anna, you're a bitch.'

'Aren't we all?' murmured Anna, admiring the golden coronet of curls. 'But you're one of the nicest.'

Felicity assumed an air of mock severity. 'Flattery, my dear Anna, will get you nowhere. I shall be nice to this Curtis Moreau since he's to be our guest, but no more than politeness demands.'

'We shall see,' said Anna darkly, and with this parting shot left the room.

In her hurry to get the evening over, since Blain would not be arriving until the following day, Felicity went down to dinner earlier than usual, to see a tall immaculate figure about to enter the lounge. He turned, and a slight smile hovered on his sardonic lips as he watched her descend the last of the stairs. There was no doubt in his mind that this deceptively lovely creature was the twin of the boy he had been asked to defend. Upon seeing him, she had descended the last stairs slowly, reluctantly, one small, slender hand on the curved balustrade, the long, graceful lines of her evening dress floating like mist above the toes of her small silver slippers. There was an untouched aura about the deep blue eyes gazing at him serenely from beneath winged brows; but it was her mouth, tenderly curved with no hint of inherent weakness, on which his eyes lingered. Her poise was touchingly regal and in no way connected with that of an older, more experienced woman.

Curtis Moreau had known many beautiful women during

his short, dynamic career, but none like this one, who looked as though she had found her own particular niche in life and was happy in it. But then so many women took up acting these days, and he remembered cynically just how good some of them could be. From his own face, set in into its usual cynical mask, no onlooker would have known that he was oddly disturbed within.

His eyes, narrowed beneath their strongly marked brows, captured and held her own as she approached. As she met that intent gaze, Felicity's heart began to beat in uneven jerks, and she had the curious feeling that the room was blacked out while the light shed a torchlike beam on the tall, loosely knit figure in the evening suit.

His thick dark hair, in spite of disciplined grooming, showed a strong tendency to wave, and the light was coaxing bronze glints in it. Her breath caught in her throat, and she was filled with a strange unaccountable shyness as she stood before him, unable to speak.

'Miss Felicity Vale-Norton?' he asked.

She nodded, and he continued in a deep, very attractive voice.

'Curtis Moreau. No doubt your father has told you I have been invited here for the weekend.' He held out his hand. 'I don't believe we've met before.'

Felicity put out her hand and managed to smile into the dark, inscrutable face so far above her own.

'No, we haven't. I hope you'll enjoy your visit,' she said quietly.

'I have a feeling that I'm going to, immensely.'

He smiled down at her after a brief handshake. It had been an impersonal one, nothing impertinent about it, but Felicity had found the contact with those cool, strong fingers most disturbing. And as they entered the lounge she was disturbingly aware of his tall, broad-shouldered frame, his bronzed and clear-cut face and the easy elegance of his long stride.

During dinner she found his male magnetism drawing her eyes in his direction against her will. And again she experienced the extraordinary strength and vitality in his gaze as their eyes met across the dinner table. Her heart gave a curious lurch and her eyes fell from his in confusion, leaving her furious with herself for allowing his presence to dominate her senses. Why should he disturb her so? No other man had ever done so to the extent that this one did.

She could see why he was successful at the bar. He was the kind of man irresistible to women of any age, and at the same time instilled confidence; one felt instinctively that he was a man one could trust. He talked with wit and humour and he had that congenital gift of assessing the value and power of words, which he used economically while making his subject interesting. He never dominated the conversation, but his presence dominated the room. No one, Felicity decided, could ignore his personality; he was so dynamic, so disturbing. She found herself hanging on to his every word as he moved easily from one subject to another.

She was not the only one who was enjoying his company. Her father had lost the look of strain he had carried since Blain's announcement of the impending divorce, and was visibly enjoying himself. He admired the brilliant brain behind his guest's shrewd perception and wisdom, and he knew he would be lucky if he could persuade him to defend his son.

As for Elvira, she responded to his charm like a flower opening its petals to the sun. He teased her in his deep disturbing voice and she laughed often at his innuendoes.

Later, Felicity said to her mother, 'Don't you agree that professional men, like doctors and barristers, are rather uncomfortable men to be with?'

Both women had returned to the lounge after dinner, leaving the two men with their wine and cigars. From her seat on the couch, Elvira looked down on the bright eyes and flushed cheeks of her daughter, who had dropped down on the white sheepskin hearthrug at her feet.

'Do you mean Curtis Moreau, or professional men in general?' she asked.

Felicity hugged her knees and stared into the blazing log fire.

'Both, I suppose. I mean ... well ... they're so cynical with experience. They give you the impression of being able to look right through you to your very soul. It's ... most unsettling, almost indecent.'

Elvira said slowly,

'Experienced men of the world usually do have that effect on the less experienced, and I should imagine Curtis Moreau is more disturbing than most. I find him extremely attractive, and I'm sure other women do too. His busy life could be responsible for the fact that he has remained a bachelor.'

Felicity digested this at some length. 'The man probably hasn't one romantic bone in his body. He's like a machine,' she said.

Elvira's voice was placid. 'You're annoyed because he didn't give you the attention during dinner that he gave to me. No, I would say he has a deep capacity for passion and feeling which he hides beneath a veneer of self-discipline. He knows all the answers, and is only prepared to go as far as he chooses.'

Suddenly, Felicity rose to her feet and paced the rug. 'Blain is an idiot to get into this mess,' she cried explosively.

Elvira laid back her neat head of natural golden hair against the cushions. The years had been kind to her and her neat, slim figure, which she invariably adorned in pastel shades, was as elegant as her daughter's.

'Blain is only human, and the best of men are selfish,' she vouchsafed. 'You'll find that out some day.'

'But not tonight,' Felicity said firmly. 'I've had a surfeit of men for one day. I'm going to bed.'

Before she went to sleep that night the aura of Curtis Moreau clung to her, and the memory of him, the intent gaze of his eyes haunted her until her eyes closed in slumber.

She was up early the next morning for her ride on Sandy. The morning was crisp and cool, with the scent of roses in the air as she turned in to the creeper-clad walls of the stable. And there he was, swinging himself up easily into the saddle of one of the Colonel's horses. He turned round, smiling, and Felicity was very aware of his virile and compelling good looks.

'Good morning, Miss Vale-Norton,' he said as Sandy moved restless hooves behind the musk-scented stable doors. 'Am I to have the pleasure of your company?'

He was immaculately and correctly turned out for the occasion in dun-coloured breeches and riding boots, his shoulders square in the well-cut jacket.

'If you can bear it,' she answered, feeling strangely lighthearted.

Her joy increased to feel Sandy beneath her, stepping out in delight when the springy turf was at last beneath his feet. That swift canter, with the morning air caressing her face and the soft thud of the horse's hooves in rhythm, was something she would never forget. The man beside her spoke little, and when he smiled she sensed an inner aloofness. I wonder what he's really like beneath all his cool reserve, she found herself thinking, and stole fugitive glances at his masculine profile.

He seemed to be deep in thought; considerate, charming and smiling down at her, he might have been miles away. No woman will ever hold him, she told herself, and was surprised that the thought had occurred to her when she had not been regarding him in that light herself.

He was an excellent horseman, sitting the saddle as though born to it.

'Do you ride often?' she asked, then felt suddenly ridiculous for asking such a question when she knew that his work could not have given him much leisure to do so.

'Not as much as I should like to,' he replied laconically. They had arrived back at the stables and Felicity slid down from the saddle into the hands he put out to hold her. His touch sent a richer colour to her face, and her breath caught in her throat. His hands were very strong and gentle.

'Thank you, Miss Vale-Norton, for a most delightful ride,' he said.

He held her slender waist for a moment, his clasp firm yet impersonal. Felicity had the feeling that he was keeping his distance as she thanked him in return.

Irritated, she assumed a lightheartedness of spirit. 'I'm hungry, I don't know about you,' she told him.

'Ravenous. Shall we have breakfast together?'

She laughed. 'Why not? We'll eat now and change later.'

So they ate their eggs and toast together. Neither of her parents put in an appearance, and they had coffee on the terrace in the sun-dappled light.

Curtis had picked a cigar from the box on the table and lighted it. After several draws from it he looked at the glowing end, then at her.

'Is this your daily routine, or do you vary your activties from day to day?' he asked. 'For instance, have you a fiancé?'

'No. I love my home,' she answered simply.

He nodded comprehendingly. 'It's certainly an enchanting place. Would you take me round it?'

Felicity hesitated for a moment, then said impulsively, 'Of course. Do you want to look around now?'

'Why not?'

Her parents came down to breakfast as they crossed the hall. The Colonel was in riding clothes.

'I see you've beaten me to it,' he said, eyes twinkling.

Elvira simply greeted them charmingly. 'Have you had

breakfast?' she asked, and smiled with no change of expression when Felicity told her they had, and were now going on a tour of the house.

She took Curtis up winding stone steps to the top of one of the twin towers, where they could look at a panoramic view of the countryside above the carved, stone edge of the battlements. And he listened intently to the stories she told of the house and its connections with Cromwell and other great names in history. His knowledge of architecture and history pleased her, and she warmed to the subject so close to her heart, her home.

'I hope I'm not boring you,' she said as they entered the long picture gallery where so many long-deceased members of the Vale-Norton family looked down at them from the panelled walls.

'On the contrary, I'm enjoying it immensely. It's only when one walks around places like this, steeped with history and tradition, that one realizes that it's man's creative beauty which endures and not the kind of ugliness with which we are surrounding ourselves in the present age.'

He lingered for some time before a picture of Blain and herself painted when they were four years old. His eyes were intent upon the angelic small faces, Felicity's large, solemn eyes and cascade of golden hair, Blain's mop of curls.

Felicity chuckled. 'Blain hates this picture of him. He says he looks too much like a girl.'

'Which explains why he's so busy proving he's not,' Curtis commented dryly. 'Tell me about him.'

'He's nice really. He's an excellent sportsman, a crack shot, first-class horseman, swims like a fish, loves rugby and can do the repairs to his car.' She laughed at his raised brows. 'Have I said enough to be going on with?'

'Enough to convince me that he's all male,' murmured her companion.

Felicity came straight to the point. She looked serious

again.

'You will . . . take on his case, won't you?' she asked with a suspicion of a tremble in her voice. 'You see, Daddy wants him to go into politics later, so it's important for someone like you to stand for him.'

He nodded. 'On the other hand,' he said slowly, 'it would do him good not to be able to extricate himself so easily this time. I'm not sure that your brother is the kind we want in politics. The son of an indulgent mother is the last candidate I would want to represent me in Parliament.'

She went pale. 'That's clever of you,' she said.

'It's part of my job to be able to see below the surface of my clients, and your brother is easy enough to read. I had a talk with him before I came down here.' He gave a slow smile, and once again she thought how very attractive he could be. 'He appeared to think his only sin was being found out.'

She looked at him hopefully. 'Does that mean you'll help him?'

'As I'm representing Mrs Staffordly, I have no other alternative,' he answered.

CHAPTER THREE

BLAIN arrived after lunch, and was shut up in the library with his father and Curtis Moreau for the rest of the afternoon. So when David Colston rang to ask her to go out for the evening to a show and dinner, Felicity accepted. His home was a matter of two miles away, and he called to collect her in his car. She saw his look of appraisal as she slipped into her seat beside him, and they sat together in silence until he reached the motorway.

'Have you missed me?' he asked with a swift glance at her delicate profile.

'Naturally.'

'How much?'

'Considerably, since Blain has been away too, on manoeuvres,' she said lightly.

'Changed your mind about what I asked you?' he asked quizzically.

'No. But need we talk about it tonight? I want to enjoy myself!' She wondered if he had heard about Blain's affair with Nora Staffordly, and concluded that it was quite likely that he had. He did not enlarge upon her remark, and she was content to rest her head back and allow the cool breeze to blow against her face.

The show they went to was a good one, with one of her old favourite film stars in the lead. She thoroughly enjoyed it, although David seemed to be a little restless. As it was Saturday night the restaurant they went to afterwards was crowded, but David had booked a table on the terrace and they dined out of doors.

It was over coffee that David's restlessness flared, and he caught her hand across the table. His face was flushed beneath the tan and he looked searchingly into her deep blue eyes.

'Felicity, you've got to marry me. I can't get away from you no matter how I try. All the time away I kept thinking about you—I can't concentrate on anything any more. Nothing makes sense to me unless you're included—I love you. Say you'll marry me.' He spoke with urgent desperation. 'I don't mean right away, if you'd rather not. But couldn't we become engaged?'

'Please, David, don't.' She rose to her feet, her thoughts going round in her head until they did not make sense. She could do worse than marry him. For all his faults he was straight and honest, and once away from his mother he might be the kind of man she wanted. Her parents would be delighted, but would she? Now that she had to make a choice for her future way of life, Felicity was frightened, too frightened to plunge headlong into something which would so deeply involve her own life and his.

Against her will her gaze was caught by his. 'I'd like to go home,' she said.

She walked ahead of him to where they had parked the car and he came up behind her.

'Felicity.' He turned her round to face him, his voice strangely humble. 'I'm sorry if I've upset you. I didn't mean to. Only having you with me this evening, looking so lovely and untouchable, made me realize how much I want you.'

She tried to be flippant, hating the idea of hurting him. 'That's the little boy in you, wanting what he can't have.'

His hands tightened painfully on her arms. 'Don't joke about it. I'm perfectly serious,' he said grimly.

'So am I. Shall we go?'

When they drew up at the door of Norton Towers, David switched off the engine and Felicity gave him her hand.

'Thanks for a pleasant evening,' she said.

But he looked down at her hand and ignored it sulkily, and she left the car to hear him grudgingly return her quiet goodnight. He drove away immediately, leaving her walking to the entrance door. Watching the tail lights of his car disappear along the drive, she turned towards the garden, feeling the need for air. Pity the evening had been spoiled, she thought; but then it had been spoiled for David too. She took a path roofed in by pergolas of roses and walked to a white marble seat where she spread out her long skirt and sat down.

She had shrugged off many proposals, but none of her suitors had the happy associations which David held for her. Maybe it was because he reminded her so much of Blain that she was so disturbed about refusing him. But while he was a stimulating and amusing companion, as a husband he would fall very short of the kind of man she wanted. As yet Felicity was not sure what she did want, but she knew it was not a man she would have to mother.

She sighed, then started as a light firm footstep sounded on the still night air. Turning her head sharply, she saw the glowing end of a cigar and then the man behind it.

'Well, well,' Curtis Moreau drawled deeply. 'Did you slide down a moonbeam to keep a rendezvous with the little people?'

It was maddening and embarrassing to find her heart going twenty to the dozen at the mockery in his voice, and she was suddenly tongue-tied. In the moonlight he looked darker and even more inscrutable than she had remembered him, with the white of his shirt contrasting sharply with his dark evening suit and tanned face.

She found her voice. 'No, just an ordinary mortal who is loath to go indoors on such a heavenly night.'

'Pity your escort had to leave so soon. He's missed the best part of the evening,' he said, lowering himself beside her at the other end of the seat.

Felicity lifted her chin. 'That's a matter of opinion,' she said defiantly.

'Indeed.' He flicked the ash from his cigar and stretched

out his legs more comfortably. 'What is he, dumb, deaf and blind?'

She clenched her hands, hating the cynical inflection, and wished idiotically that she was as experienced as he was in life. The knowledge that she was not his kind of woman not only infuriated her, but also made her feel inexperienced and naïve. His mocking amusement hurt in an inexplicable way.

Her voice slid on ice. 'As you are a guest I can't very well show my resentment at your unwarranted interference, but I would remind you that I am my own mistress and I am answerable to no one.'

'Are you?' he answered, quite unabashed. 'Rather cold up there on your pedestal, isn't it? Lonely, too.' Suddenly his hand shot out to grip her arm beneath the flimsy evening wrap. 'You're cold, you little idiot. What are you trying to do, catch a chill? Come on, you're going indoors.'

He dropped the butt end of his cigar and ground it with his heel. Then he pulled her to her feet. It was true that Felicity had been feeling the nip in the night air moments ago, but now it seemed that his light firm touch had sent an exhilarating heat through her body, flowing like a heady wine through her veins. Angry and dismayed that he should affect her so, she walked beside him in silence, her head averted.

'I was in the Guards when I was younger,' he vouchsafed. 'We might have met had you not been in the schoolroom at the time.'

She lifted her chin. 'I'm twenty-five.'

He raised an attractive brow. 'You look about eighteen.'

'I haven't your experience,' she retorted.

'True, nor my years. I'm thirty-one.'

Felicity imagined him in the uniform of the Queen's Guard, the hussar type, dark blue fringed with yellow, scarlet-striped, topped by a busby—an outfit well suited to his lean, wide-shouldered frame. How often had he strolled with a girl in the gloaming of a summer evening away from the musk-scented stables to the chivalrous clink of spurs and the scent of honeysuckle from creeper-clad walls?

For some reason the thought gave her pain and she wanted to hurt him, if that were possible.

'What happened?' she asked caustically. 'Did they throw you out?'

He gave a deep-throated chuckle.

'You sound as though you were hoping they did,' he said with cool amusement, and she felt a little ashamed. After all, he was there at her father's invitation, and her anger was quite unwarranted since he had been concerned about her being cold.

She glanced at his profile from the corner of her eye, the masculine nose that would give character to any face, the firmly cut lips curved humorously, and she wondered at his thoughts as he pushed his hands into his pockets and slowed down his stride to accommodate her shorter one.

'I resigned my commission,' he went on, and looked down at her his expression suddenly grave. 'My father was wrongly accused of falsifying the accounts of one of his companies, and the fool of an advocate blundered and failed to get him an acquittal. My father died from a heart attack brought on by shock. He never heard the truth come out and his name cleared. That was the reason I studied for the bar. I took silk four years ago.'

They had reached the house and Felicity wanted to say she was sorry, but he did not give her the opportunity. She was on the verge of speaking when he gave a cool very brief bow.

'Goodnight, Miss Vale-Norton. You mustn't stay longer in the cold air. Take a warm drink before you go to bed, preferably hot milk with a little whisky. Sleep well.'

Sunday passed pleasantly and swiftly, beginning with an early ride when Felicity was accompanied by her brother and Curtis Moreau. Blain had become an ardent admirer of the man who was going to represent him.

'I wish I had his brain,' he said to Felicity with brotherly candour. They were walking to the tennis courts, racquets in hand, after lunch.

'You probably have the equivalent. His is razor sharp because he's disciplined it that way.'

Felicity swung her racquet negligently, looking down absently at her long slender legs in white tennis shorts. For some reason she was back on ice where Curtis Moreau was concerned.

Blain looked at her thoughtfully. 'You don't approve of him, do you?'

'I neither approve nor disapprove,' she shrugged.

He appraised the blue scarf tied round her head and knotted at the side of her slender neck, the open-necked cream silk blouse tailored to fit the small pointed contours of her pretty bust, the small waist and slender hips.

'I bet he approves of you,' he said mildly.

They had reached the tennis courts, and Felicity hated to think that they were in full view of the lawns in front of the house where Curtis was talking to her parents. He was leaning negligently against one of the stone pillars supporting the terrace, at one with the strangeness of his surroundings. The fact that he seemed in command of any situation served to set off her feeling of antagonism.

'There I don't agree.' She flexed her fingers before gripping her racquet more firmly. 'I don't think Curtis Moreau approves of either of us. Shall I serve?'

She moved round to the opposite side of the net, deliberately presenting a slim back to the watchers on the terrace.

For the next quarter of an hour or so she became engrossed in a brisk game. Blain was on form, having loaded his troubles on Curtis Moreau's broad shoulders. Then they changed places and she moved round to the other side of the net to see her parents and their guest watching, engrossed in their playing.

Bareheaded, Curtis Moreau still leaned indolently against the stone pillar, his subtle arrogance giving an air to the casual sweater and linen slacks he wore and making them seem correct.

Felicity allowed her glance to rest momentarily upon her audience, then concentrated upon the game. In spite of deliberately doing her best, her own cool front began to shrivel and her movements were off cue. She was leaping to stop a particularly strong volley when her foot slipped, and she fell sideways on the hard court.

Instantly, Blain leaped over the net to bend over her anxiously.

'That was some dive,' he said sympathetically. 'Are you hurt?'

She tried gallantly to smile, feeling shaken and slightly sick as he placed an arm about her shoulders.

'I'll survive,' she assured him weakly, trying not to wince at the painful twinge in her elbow.

The next moment Curtis Moreau was there, bending over her and straightening her slim, golden legs, feeling for injuries with cool impersonal fingers. Moisture gathered on her temples and she gave him a pale fleeting smile.

'I'm all right,' she said.

He looked at her pallor and slid his arms beneath her. 'I'm going to carry you indoors,' he said. 'You look shaken and you need to take it quietly for a while.'

Before Blain could offer to help he had swept her up strongly into his arms and was striding purposefully towards the house.

'She's only shaken, but I think she'll benefit from a little rest,' he told the Colonel and Elvira, who were on their feet as they approached the terrace.

Felicity, who was recovering her breath, smiled at them reassuringly.

'I'm all right,' she said. 'No bones broken.'

Her parents nodded dazedly, and watched them go through the doorway into the house. It was odd that Anna seemed to be nowhere about when Curtis mounted the stairs; or perhaps she was busy in another part of the house. In a way, Felicity was glad Anna was missing. Somehow she would feel embarrassed beneath that critical, kindly gaze in the arms of a strange man. At least, he was strange for what little she knew about him. But she was learning fast, learning that he had the power to set her pulses racing madly, and that she could have rested in his arms forever.

The relief when he laid her down gently on her bed was overwhelming; for a few seconds the room spun round and she felt sick. She lay limply allowing the bed to take her weight as dew gathered on her temples. Her hands were moist and clammy, and she shivered.

Curtis looked enormous as he bent over her in a wavering mist, and she wished he would go away. He did. Then he was back with a tray and a cup of sweet tea. By this time the faintness and nausea had gone, and she managed to push herself up into a sitting position as he entered the room.

His glance at her was keen as he put down the tray.

'How are you feeling?' he asked, pouring out the tea.

'Much better, thanks. I'm glad you brought me to my room. I thought you were making an unnecessary fuss. It must have been the violent way I fell, it kind of upset my balance. I'm fine now, though.'

'You will be when you've had a drink.' He pushed the pillows closer to her back and gave her the cup of tea, then he sat down on the side of the bed and grinned at her. 'You certainly put an enormous amount of energy into your game.' He rubbed his clean-shaven chin reflectively. 'I had the idea that you were taking me for the ball, hence the vicious attack. Was I right?'

Felicity sipped the tea, not in the least surprised at his keen perception. Her sinews tightened as he waited for an answer; suddenly the air was fraught with electric waves and they seemed to be coming to her from him. She could not speak at first for the beating of her heart. But Felicity was not one for not speaking the truth. She smiled waveringly, a charming dimple in the curve of her cheek.

'I told my mother last evening after dinner that I found professional people, such as doctors and Q.C.s, very embarrassing to be with. They're not only too discerning, they are also arrogant. You are both.'

He raised his brows. 'So I was right. You were hitting out at me? Fine. I like spirit in a woman—shows she's alive. Neither a horse nor a woman are any good without it.' He grasped her left arm gently and, bending his head sideways, examined her grazed elbow. 'Does it hurt?' he asked.

Felicity shook her head. 'Not much.'

His tongue was in his cheek. 'That, my dear Miss Vale-Norton, is the understatement of the year. There's gravel in the wound and it has an angry look. I bet it's hurting like hell.' He looked round the room. 'Have you any dressings handy?'

She nodded. 'In the bathroom cabinet.'

He strode across the room into the bathroom and was back in record time, armed with a towel, soaped face-cloth smelling of antiseptic and an adhesive dressing.

'This is going to sting a little at first. Just dwell on the relief from pain two minutes from now.'

His touch was extraordinarily gentle, and he glanced up at her face as he cleaned out the wound. Felicity felt no pain, for she was too conscious of the man treating her so deftly. He had, as it were, stormed into her neat, well-ordered existence with the cataclysmic charm and unexpectedness of an entirely new experience. Until now her life had not brought her into the company of young men of his calibre; from their first meeting he had excited her brain and imagination. She was feeling odd again, only this

42

time it was an oddness resulting from some kind of exquisite terror. Her breath caught suddenly as she wanted to reach out and touch the firm springy growth of his hair, to let her hand slide down the curve of his tanned face. Then she knew that her terror was fear of him. He alone had the power to make her feel fright . . . and love.

With a wild exultant leap of her pulses she knew that this man, whom she had known for little more than two days, had taken possession of her as surely as if they had slept together. Effortlessly, he had stepped in and taken her with all that casual arrogance she had so bitterly resented, but which now made her clay in his hands.

She loved him. It seemed incredible. The quick currents of electricity rioting through her veins at the touch of his hands was the kind of feeling poets raved about. And it had happened to her.

'There, how does that feel?'

He fixed the waterproof adhesive dressing with a last gentle pat and smiled at her. Felicity shook herself from her thoughts with a sense of shock. But if something cataclysmic had happened to her it had not affected him, for he regarded her lazily with narrow-eyed charm.

'Very comfortable, thanks,' she replied, and he moved from the bed to return the things he had used to the bathroom.

Bemused, she looked around the room, seeking some change. Since her own life had changed so drastically it did not seem possible that there was no difference in the still quiet room, with its flowers and feminine furnishings which were so much a part of a woman's domain.

Anna came in before Curtis returned from the bathroom, and Felicity had an idea her look of surprise was assumed for the occasion.

'What's happened?' she queried.

'Miss Vale-Norton fell on the tennis courts and grazed her elbow,' Curt followed his deep voice from the bathroom. 'She's resting.'

'I see,' said Anna, taking in Felicity's scarlet cheeks and starry eyes. She took in the tea tray thoughtfully. 'Would you like some fresh tea?'

Curt said, 'No, thanks. I'm leaving Miss Vale-Norton to rest.'

'Now that is what I call a man,' Anna said when he had gone.

Felicity never did remember much of the rest of that day. After a rest she took a bath and dressed for dinner, sensing only an occasional twinge in her injured elbow. Anna was noncommittal as she helped her to dress, but there was a decided gleam in her eye as she put out the white silk dress, demure in its simplicity, with its Empire bodice and long full sleeves. The thick eyebrows rose a trifle as Felicity allowed the dress to fall over her slim form without comment. Usually she chose her own dress and was very decided in what she was going to wear. Tonight, however, her thoughts were far away.

It was only when she was on her way downstairs that she came back with a jerk to the present, for Curtis Moreau was taking the stairs two at a time towards her. He halted upon seeing her, and her heart gave a curious tilt. Her eyes fell from his—she was painfully aware of herself, and of him. A wave of colour washed over her face as she came slowly down the last steps to where he stood. Again Felicity was conscious of the strength and magnetism of his personality. She found herself looking at him with new eyes, knowing that the magical mystery and ecstasy of love had passed her by until now. It was one of those inevitable things, as sure as the laws of nature, yet swift, terrifying and overwhelming but with the lovely simplicity of all things natural.

He said, with a gleam of amusement in his eyes, 'How is the elbow, and how are you feeling?'

'All right to both,' she answered demurely. 'Thanks again for your kindness.'

He expressed his delight as they walked down the rest of the stairs and across the hall into the lounge where her parents were waiting along with Blain. As all three had been to her room to see her soon after Curtis had gone downstairs after dressing her elbow, they asked solicitously how she was feeling and her father poured drinks.

All through dinner, Curtis Moreau emanated a magnetism to Felicity that was irresistible, and impressed the rest of the family with his easy charm, her mother especially. Elvira hung on to his every word with a look in her eye that her daughter had never seen before, almost coquettish.

So the evening wore on, with Felicity feeling a little bewildered because Curtis Moreau, while charmingly affable and courteous, kept everything impersonal. On an acute sense of disappointment and the feeling that she had been steeling herself against something which was not likely to happen, Felicity left the dining room eventually with her mother, who went to make a promised phone call to a sick friend.

Slowly Felicity strolled out on to the terrace, and breathed deeply of the scented night air. Her life here at Norton Towers was happy and uncomplicated, and she had been crazily happy with Blain for a companion. Why then should she want it altered? Curtis Moreau's attractions lay in the fact that he was different from the other young men of her acquaintance. She had simply lost her head over his little act of chivalry; it was no more than that.

How long she stood there, clinging again poignantly to the past after that rather ecstatic look into the future, Felicity did not know, but she gave a violent start as the aroma of a fine cigar drifted along towards her. Gripping the stone edge of the balustrade, she kept perfectly still, hoping that he would not turn his head and see her. Her white dress was hardly a camouflage in the soft gloaming of the summer night, and there was a pause while he dispensed with the butt of his cigar.

Seconds later he had come to a halt beside her to say quietly, 'I'm leaving tonight for London, Miss Vale-Norton.' His smile was wholly charming. 'May I thank you for making my visit a very happy and memorable one? I've thoroughly enjoyed myself.'

He put out his hand and her heart gave a curious lurch. 'So soon?' she said, turning slowly to look up into his enigmatic gaze. He would reveal nothing of his feelings, this man who had so steeped himself into disciplinary action that his heart was automatic as well.

'I must.' His fingers closed around her small hand with gentle firmness as he went on in a less impersonal tone, 'Will you walk with me to my car?'

He released her hand and she walked with him along the terrace.

'You have a beautiful place here,' he commented pleasantly. 'I live in chambers.'

'Have you no family?' she exclaimed, chiding herself for feeling sorry for this polished automaton.

'I have a mother who lives in Paris. I also have an excellent *homme à tout faire* in my ménage named Henri.' He spoke with the careless arrogance of a man whose life set out deliberately to please him. Felicity felt suddenly shut out.

'Are you French?' she asked, for something to say.

'My father was French. My mother is English. She has lived in Paris since my father died,' he answered laconically.

Felicity found herself wondering what kind of a woman his mother was, and how much or how little other women had counted in his life. There obviously had been other women, since he had that congenital magnetism that insensibly draws and captures them. They had reached his car, and he leaned against it negligently as he spoke again.

'Will you dine with me one evening?' he asked casually.

46

Taken aback, she hesitated. Then, because the thought of not seeing him again was unbearable, she nodded.

'I'd love to,' she answered.

'Shall we say Thursday evening? I'll come down to collect you at around six o'clock as it's an hour's run from London; that should get us there in good time for a show and dinner afterwards.' He straightened and looked down at her quizzically. 'And don't you think you could call me Curt, Felicity?'

Again she nodded, and felt him take her hand, saw his teeth white in a grin.

'Goodbye until Thursday, and let Anna put you a fresh dressing on that elbow tomorrow. Take care.'

CHAPTER FOUR

FELICITY slept fitfully that night, and awoke unrefreshed. Her dreams had been vaguely disturbing, and the uneasy conflict feathering through them remained with her when she awoke to see Anna drawing the curtains.

'Lovely morning,' said Anna.

Felicity stretched her arms above her head sleepily and blinked.

'Curtis Moreau asked me to dine with him on Thursday evening.' She smiled, feeling pleasure at the speaking of his name.

Anna placed the tray before her, her face enigmatic. 'And you accepted?'

'Of course. Are you surprised?'

A shrug. 'You would have been a fool not to. He's your kind of man. Like you in a way—he has a will of his own and does exactly what he pleases.'

Felicity bristled. 'Maybe, but he won't do what he likes with me.'

'That's what you think.'

'Anna!' She pushed herself up more firmly behind the tray and glared. 'What's got into you this morning? You're smiling. Does that mean you approve?'

'I wish I was young again,' said Anna.

Felicity poured out her tea. 'So beneath that starched front beats a romantic heart! Well, let me tell you something. A man will have to be something special to make me change my way of life.'

'Curtis Moreau is.'

Felicity sipped her tea, found it too hot and coughed painfully.

'He's only a man,' she cried. 'Really! Why do people

assume that all spinsters are mad to get married?' irritably. 'I like things as they are. Why does one have to give up one thing for another?'

'Because you can't have your cake and eat it,' Anna said, and with this piece of wisdom left the room.

Felicity waited for Thursday to come with delicious expectancy. It was a silent and quivering waiting which she hugged to herself jealously, but when Wednesday evening arrived she knew a feeling of fear. Her breath caught suddenly at the thought of meeting him again, and the colour flooded her cheeks. She had been playing tennis that afternoon with one of her old school friends and the dressing on her almost-healed elbow seemed to bring Curt very near. She had been alarmed to discover how much he had dominated her thoughts. He had robbed her of her own identity, and she was afraid. Her parents were dining out that night and she had dined alone, and so her fears had mounted until there was an irresistible urge to leave the house to seek clear thinking in the cool night air.

Curt was the dominant male, a man of implacable demands which would take all from her. Away from the house filled with the memory of him, Felicity tried to think rationally. What exactly did she want from life? A husband and children? But not with David Colston, she told herself, for it was not love she felt for him. Theirs would be a lifeless, mundane marriage with no flames of passion; with Curt life would be very different. The instant leap of her pulses at the thought of him verified that.

But just as David would demand too little, Curt would take too much, he would take all. He would make her his in a way that would make her a mere appendage of himself— her treacherous heart leapt at the thought, in delicious terror. And she would give and go on giving, because she would not be able to resist him. If she accepted the date with him, Felicity knew with an inborn feminine intuition that it was a decision that would affect her whole life.

She walked through the grounds seeing nothing of her surroundings, deaf and blind to everything because of Curt. Why should he do this to me? she asked herself. And the answer came. They were akin to each other. Were she to never see him again, he would always be there in her heart. She would never be free of him again.

Felicity had reached panic stations by the time she returned to the house. It was now or never, she thought, and made blindly for the telephone after looking up Curt's number.

After what seemed an age a deep-voiced individual, raising no question as to his maleness, answered.

He said, 'I'm afraid Mr Moreau is out. Can I give him a message?'

She told him then that she would not be able to keep the dinner date for the following evening, and apologized. Putting down the phone, she had to sit down very suddenly, having gone weak at the knees. It took quite some time to pull herself together, and she began to make plans.

She would be crafty and let Anna think she was going to her date. She was sure to come to help her to dress for the occasion, so that was what she must do. Felicity decided to dress as though she were going, but leave the house in the car half an hour before Curt would be due. Then if Curt, who she was sure had never been stood up by a girl before, suddenly decided to call for an explanation, she would be out.

Thursday was never-ending, and it was a strain for her to behave normally in case Anna grew suspicious when the time came for her to get ready. She chose a blue gown, the one she would have chosen for her dinner date.

It was a caftan decorated with gold embroidery, and the colour, so flattering to her golden hair, deepened the blue of her eyes. Anna, who had taken the golden hair back with a

50

narrow band of matching material, surveyed her, well satisfied. 'The triple link of pearls with the matching pearl and diamond earrings, I think,' she said. 'Then you are ready.'

Felicity, silent, let her have her way. She could not have cared less that her nails were the same delicate pink as her lips and that she was chic and impeccable. As Anna fussed around her, arranging this, adjusting that, she looked at the exquisite gold watch on her wrist.

'I'm sure Mr Moreau doesn't mean you to drive up to London alone,' Anna said, going round Felicity's slim shoulders with the minute soft clothes-brush for any stray hairs. 'He's not that kind of man. I should wait a little longer if I were you; no sense in rushing off and missing him. Besides, some men like helpless girls, they appeal to their protective instinct.'

Panic rose in Felicity's throat. 'He probably knows I've driven up to London hundreds of times,' she said crossly. 'Besides, he wasn't sure whether he could get away on time. He might be in court until the last minute.'

She was rather proud of the last remark, for it sounded more than feasible. But the older woman was at the window like a shot at the sound of a car drawing up below on the gravel.

'Like to bet?' she said succinctly. 'Right on time.'

'I beg your pardon?' Felicity croaked on a sense of shock. 'Who's right on time?'

Anna, it seemed, was being deliberately obtuse. 'You were right, it looks as though Mr Moreau was unable to call for you.' A pause while she peered through the window. 'His car is here, but a strange man is getting out. He looks rather pompous and very correct. I'd say it was his valet ... Henri, I think you said.'

Felicity closed her eyes and sat up stiffly in her chair at the dressing table. 'I didn't,' she answered. 'How ... did you know Curt had a valet?'

Anna digested this. Then she said slowly, 'Come to think of it, Henri rang up this morning, introduced himself and enquired if you had changed your mind about this evening. He babbled some story about you telephoning last night cancelling the arrangement.'

Felicity surfaced from a sense of shock. 'You ... you never told me. I never....'

Anna cut in calmly, 'That's what I said. You must have had your dates mixed up. No girl in her right mind would stand Curtis Moreau up on a date. And I'm sure I told you about it this morning.'

'But, Anna ... you didn't ... I....'

But Anna was not listening. 'You mustn't keep the man waiting,' she said. 'Here's your evening bag, and I've put a clean hankie in. Have a good time.'

Before she could protest, Felicity found herself being piloted downstairs to the waiting car and Henri. Henri was a thick-set man of indeterminate age, composed, non-garrulous and utterly self-effacing. Felicity could imagine him moving, silent, light-footed and mercilessly efficient, through Curt's domain.

He stood by the open door of the car, not very tall, with a Latin look about him; dapper, neatly dressed, dark hair sleeked back from a sallow skin and brown eyes. His eyebrows lifted in a look so full of startled appraisal that Felicity bristled. Then he was giving a slight bow with the click of chivalrous heels, lowering dark eyes sparkling with delight.

'À votre service, madame,' he said in even, courteous tones. 'Mr Curtis Moreau has been delayed, and I have been dispatched to take you to await him at his chambers.'

Feeling a little strange, she sank into the back seat of the immaculate car and remembered with a swift pang her telephone call of the previous evening cancelling the engagement. Had the astute Henri told Curt about it, or had he carried out the whole operation keeping strictly neutral?

She felt a tingle of annoyance about the way the whole thing had been manoeuvred between the aggravating man taking his seat behind the wheel and Anna. For two pins she would get out of the car and send him back alone. Then, realizing how absurd the situation was, she relaxed.

The next hour went like a breeze, or was it the car? All too soon they had reached Lincolns Inn, where Henri became part of the cultured aura as he drove the car into a cobbled courtyard bright with geraniums in tubs. Felicity's heart began to beat in thick heavy strokes as Henri escorted her through a Saxon arched doorway to a suite of rooms on the first floor.

There she was shown into a room of comfortable padded leather and rich dark wood, the atmosphere of which sent all manner of turbulent feelings through her. Henri seated her suavely and, pouring out a glass of sherry, handed it to her with a supercilious little bow.

'Madame will not have to wait long,' he assured her in the same suave tones. 'Perhaps a little music, or is there anything else Madame requires?'

Felicity blushed furiously beneath his searching gaze.

'No, thanks. I'm quite comfortable.'

She was angry with herself for being so flustered when there was no need to be. It was not until he had left the room that she began to relax. She sipped her sherry for something to do and felt it run through her veins like fire, dissolving her tenseness until her shoulders relaxed and the muscles of her neck and face became less rigid.

Every second waiting for Curt was like an hour, and to relieve the tedium of waiting, she finished her sherry and rose to take a closer look at the pictures adorning the walls of the room. One in particular held her attention, a colourful hunting scene in oils. The poor unfortunate fox reminded her of herself, especially as one of the pink-coated riders chasing it looked remarkably like Curt.

And so Curt, opening the door at that precise moment,

saw her profile, the fine chiselling of her nose with its delicately wilful tilt, the tender lurking humour of her mouth and the graceful lines of her blue-clad form. His eyes were caught in the gleaming silk of her hair cascading down on to her shoulders like molten gold, and suddenly he collided with the shattering blue of her eyes as she turned her head.

To him it was a revelation which staggered him. Almost without volition he found himself quoting poetry, softly, mockingly as he closed the door and leaned back against it nonchalantly.

> 'A girl in blue.
> How shall I greet her?
> I've waited all my life
> to meet her.
> She is scared, I think,
> as I draw near
> and trembles
> with a girlish fear.
> Her eyes deep blue, pools
> in summer sun,
> implore me wildly
> to be gone.
> But I will tarry
> and tell her now.
> I've taken a vow
> to know her.'

Felicity listened entranced, and without realizing quite what was happening, suddenly found her doubts being charmed away. Grudgingly, she admitted that he was certainly a delightful man, and had an enchanting voice. Her heart lifted. She was going out to dine with a delightfully handsome and—she knew—devastatingly charming man who found her equally attractive. Fully confident now and revelling in the stirring sense of adventure ahead, she said with a smile, 'Does one person ever really know another?'

His eyes narrowed as he answered in that voice loaded with charm which instinct told her masked an iron will.

'I intend to know you better. Do you mind?'

He looked at her enquiringly. He had lunged away from the door, and was standing before her without seeming to have moved. He had changed into evening dress, and she noticed again the quiet perfection of his clothes and the air with which he wore them.

'Why should I?' she asked with a smile.

'That's what I would like to know. Why did you telephone last evening cancelling our date?'

His voice was low and dangerously soft. Her heart gave a sudden lurch, and she lowered her eyes as a wave of colour crept up beneath her clear skin, leaving her furious with herself for not being prepared for the obvious question.

'I don't honestly know,' she admitted after a pause. 'Unless it was because you are so self-assured. You Q.C.s are a species who have quite an advantage over us less experienced women.' She moistened dry lips. 'You give me the impression of being intense in everything you say and do; a poor girl wouldn't have a chance if you decided to storm her defences. And you know all the answers.'

'Are you afraid of me?' he demanded, borrowing her forthrightness.

She nodded. 'Something like that.' His frown made her add quickly, 'Have I annoyed you?'

Curt smiled slightly. 'I'm managing to bear it with a degree of fortitude,' he answered dryly. 'This is most enlightening. Do go on.'

Felicity lifted her eyes. He was laughing at her, but she knew it was not so much at her as with her.

Her mouth curved demurely. 'I am being rather idiotic, aren't I? Ungrateful too, since you're doing so much for Blain.'

He said quietly, 'I want no gratitude for doing my job.

You owe me nothing. I would like to say one thing on the other subject. You're right when you say my demands of any woman would be high. But while I would expect her to give I would give as well.' He placed firm fingers beneath her elbow. 'Shall we go?'

The evening was a complete success. The show they went to was a good one and dinner afterwards was equally enjoyable. It occurred to Felicity when he was driving her home that if he was a man of many words in court, outside he was a man of few. He never bored her with trying to impress, even though he must have been well aware that his appearance was enough to add more than ten per cent to the cost of any meal he had out. And she adored his sense of humour.

At her door he refused to come in for a drink, because he had work to do on a case on returning to his chambers.

Felicity nodded comprehendingly and extended her hand. 'Thank you for a delightful evening,' she said.

He held it firmly. 'When can I see you again? To-morrow?'

She shook her head. 'Not tomorrow.'

'Saturday?' he persisted.

He still held her hand and her heart was racing. There was no resisting his charm.

'All right,' she replied, suddenly breathless. Then, before he could say anything further, she quickly withdrew her hand from his warm clasp and went indoors.

Deep sound sleep eluded her that night. Curt's image was forever before her and she wished with all her heart that she had never met him. Until he came she had been resigned to her old way of life and recalled with an aching heart the lovely tranquil days at Norton Towers, the long, leisurely days of summer with meals outdoors and the exhilarating canters on Sandy on winter mornings with the snow glistening like fairy icing on trees and shrubs.

She was awake and heavy-eyed when Anna came with

her breakfast tray eager to hear about her night out, but she retold it as gaily as she could. The dark shadows beneath her eyes, however, did not escape Anna's keen gaze.

'You look peaky,' she observed with concern, 'it's all that worry over Blain. Don't worry over him. He'll fall on his feet, as he always does.'

At eleven o'clock that morning a spray of dark red roses arrived. The attached card in Curt's firm masculine hand quickened Felicity's pulses, and Anna put them in a vase in her room where they made a vivid splash of colour against the pale walls. Looking at them, Felicity felt a cold numbness in her limbs, and her will seemed to have been bludgeoned. The next two days before she was due to meet him again were the longest she had ever lived through. Try as she would, she found it impossible to concentrate upon anything for long without his image intruding. She raged in vain at her utter helplessness against the battery of his charm, and could not understand the longing for him that had taken hold of her—a longing she had never felt for any man before. Furthermore, she was loath to confide in Anna, recognizing it as an important issue in her life and one that she had to decide for herself.

Felicity felt instinctively that Curt was not the kind of man to indulge in idle affairs; a man in his position would be very selective where women were concerned. With a pang, she realized what she had missed through not being close to her mother. It would have been a relief to confide in her and have the benefit of her advice. But she knew Elvira would see it not as a problem but as a splendid match for her only daughter.

So the time went on. She was ready in her room when his car drew up at the door.

'He's here,' said Anna, turning from the window to survey Felicity's slender quivering figure with unfeigned delight. Her dress, in delicate pink chiffon, gave her an ethereal look as though mortal hands had not touched it.

The skirt was composed of layers of chiffon falling softly from her small waist. Her creamy shoulders rose as delicately smooth as flower petals above the swathed bodice, and her eyes were deep blue bewildered pools.

'You look ravishing,' said Anna, going forward quickly to pick up the white ermine evening jacket. 'He's come himself,' she whispered conspiratorially, and lifted her eyes heavenwards. 'Wow! What a man!'

Felicity picked up her evening bag, waited a few moments while her pulses slowed down, then went downstairs. Curt stood by the car, looking carelessly elegant and inscrutable in evening dress. He came forward immediately on seeing her, and after a murmured greeting opened the car door.

The inside of the car was roomy and fresh, the hide upholstery well-sprung and comfortable. Felicity felt a certain solace in not having to sit too near to him on the wide seat, and she was silent as he swung the car round on the drive. His long firm fingers were relaxed and easy on the wheel. He drove as she had expected him to, with the confidence of a man who would excel in whatever he set out to do.

'Miss me?' he asked, casting a glance at her quiet profile.

'I could ask the same of you,' she replied demurely.

'And I'd tell you. I've missed you.'

Felicity looked down at her hands, clasped loosely in her lap. He had said what she wanted him to say, yet she was still unwilling to become involved. His nearness suffocated her. He was too dynamic, too overwhelming, and why did he have to have that deep, enchanting voice? But only the deep throbbing of her heart answered her, her treacherous heart that was so ready to leap at the sound of his voice, his nearness.

'I hope you don't mind,' he went on. 'We're going to dine with a colleague of mine this evening, Judge Greatman. I believe you know him well.'

She relaxed a little and said quietly, 'He's a great friend

of ours. I've known him since I was a little girl.'

In her mind's eye, Felicity was seeing a middle-aged thick-set man of kindly mien and patient countenance. At his dinner parties one invariably met many famous and distinguished people.

At dinner she was seated between Curt and a well-known writer whom she had longed to meet, and she divided her attention between them, listening silently and intelligently to their conversation. It pleased her that Curt grew gradually cooler in his conversation as the writer became almost amorous.

'You are the sort of woman I very rarely meet,' he murmured into her small pink ear, 'beautiful and intelligent, with that rare gift of knowing how to listen. When can I see you again?'

It was Curt who answered for her. Curtly, abruptly, he said with a proprietorial glance at her flushed face, 'The lady is already spoken for.'

'Delighted to have had your company this evening, Felicity,' the Judge said kindly on their departure. 'Give my regards to your parents.' He cast a droll look at the tall figure of Curt beside her. 'One thing I like about my parties, I meet such nice people. You, Curt, have known many beautiful women and had your quota of affairs, but tonight you've excelled yourself—you'll never meet anyone who will come up to this little girl here. I've known her since she was so high, so take care of her.'

Curt was very quiet on the way back to Norton Towers. At her door he was already out of the car opening her door and, before she could speak, he said, 'Thanks for an enchanting evening,' and kissed her firmly on her softly parted lips. 'I'd like you to go to Paris with me next weekend to meet my mother. I'll telephone to let you know when I shall be coming to pick you up.'

He was behind the wheel and down the drive while she stood there with a strange paralysis in all her joints, watch-

· ing his car disappear from view.

The unexpected touch of his firm, cool lips had revived all her misgivings and increased them, so that she went to her room in a fever of uncertainty.

They went to Paris on Friday evening. Felicity, seated beside Curt in the plane, refused to dwell upon the idea that he was taking her to Paris for his mother's approval. But the thought persistently pushed its way through her consciousness and, in an effort to forget it, she concentrated on the continental weekend ahead with Curt in the most romantic city on earth.

Soon she would be seeing with him the lovely Champs Elysées, the distant sweep of the Place de la Concorde and the beautiful Sacré Coeur set like a crown on the hill of Montmartre. Curt, she knew, would be the ideal companion. Dreamily she cast a sideways look as he sat relaxed beside her, a big brown man whom few women could resist. Already he dominated her until her will had become a malleable thing in his strong, well-cared-for brown hands. He had come into her life unexpectedly, and as unexpectedly had completely filled it.

Travelling with Curt was simple and relaxing; he saw to all her comforts as naturally and easily as he manipulated anything else. Everyone responded to his courteous demands and devastating smile with a grin of acknowledgement. And the air hostesses had gazed upon him dewyeyed.

It was seven-forty when the plane touched down at Beauvais and they collected the car Curt had hired to take them to Paris.

'We're meeting Mother at her favourite hotel in Paris,' Curt told her with a mocking smile of amusement at her heightened colour.

The journey to Paris took most of the next two hours, with Felicity trying not to picture what his mother would be like. People were never how you pictured them anyway, she told herself, hoping that she would not be disappointed.

Madame Moreau came into the hotel foyer a little out of breath—the epitome of French elegance in a Claude Rivière suit. Slender, chic and soignée, she approached them gracefully with outstretched hands, and Felicity felt the impact of her warm personality and charm. An exquisite gold watch studded with diamonds gleamed on her slender wrist, toning with the diamond and pearl necklace and earrings. Her brown hair had only a sprinkling of grey and her voice was seductively low-pitched.

'Curt!' she cried. 'How lovely to see you!'

He bent his head to kiss the perfumed cheek, so smooth and round with scarcely a wrinkle to mar it. Then he grinned down into the brown eyes which had not lost the brilliance of youth.

'You look younger each time I see you,' he teased, and turned to Felicity who had hung back. Taking her arm he drew her forward. 'Mother, this is Felicity.'

Felicity was aware of the subtle fragrance of eau de Cologne as Madame Moreau leaned forward to kiss her.

'I'm so happy to meet you,' she said, and she laughed with sheer pleasure, a throaty chuckle full of warmth, before stepping back to look at her. 'Why, Curt, she is *ravissante*!'

'I agree,' he answered with a mocking smile for Felicity. Then he was arming them both out of the foyer to where his mother had parked her car.

'It's naughty of Curt not to tell me about you,' said his mother as they drove away from the kerb. 'I had no idea that I was in for such a pleasant surprise.'

Curt had put both of them in the back of the car and had taken the wheel himself. Madame Moreau's warm friendliness had put Felicity instantly at her ease, and she found herself wishing she had known her husband. Like her son she was vital, intelligent and charming with a distinctive personality, the impact of which made itself felt. She listened with lively interest while Felicity told her something of her life at Norton Towers. Then she shook her head.

'Country life would never do for me,' she said in her delicious husky voice, 'I'm a city sparrow. I was born and bred in London. I hate country tweeds and slogging along muddy lanes in sturdy shoes. I like elegant and gracious living, the theatres, the night life, furs and jewellery and living in Paris.'

Felicity nodded comprehendingly. 'It wouldn't do for us all to be alike. I like city life too, but I love my home life very much.' She smiled, knowing that they had one thing in common, their love for the wide-shouldered, dark-haired Curt.

They continued to talk happily together, and presently Curt turned off a tree-lined avenue into a courtyard with walls covered by Virginia creeper. White shutters at the windows gave a festive air to the villa set in a garden.

'You'll feel at home here, Felicity,' said Madame Moreau, and gestured to an archway in the creeper-clad wall giving a glimpse of the gardens beyond. 'We have a kitchen garden and a rose garden as well. The latter is very romantic; we have a cupid on a fountain.'

She laughed with delight at Felicity's blush and Curt, stopping the car, turned to ask what the joke was.

'It's just my fun,' his mother answered, and winked at Felicity, a wink that bound them together for all time.

Inside the villa one felt the influence of the charming garden. The main salon had walls of pale grey with French tapestry on two walls; sofas, chairs and curtains were covered in a pattern cretonne in pink, green and gold set amidst Chinese porcelain and superb French period furniture. Everywhere Felicity saw the feminine touch which makes a house a home.

The guest room to which Madame Moreau escorted Felicity was also very charming. The canopied bed had blue-tasselled cretonne drapes of roses on a cream ground.

Curtains and Regency tub chairs were upholstered to match, and the whole effect, set against blue ceiling and carpet with cream walls, was enchanting. The scent of roses set about the room in crystal vases was refreshingly sweet, and Felicity gazed around with sparkling eyes.

'Do you like it?' asked Madame Moreau.

'Very much.' Felicity walked to the tall windows to look out on to the garden.

'Are you in love with my son?'

Felicity spun round startled. 'I ... I don't. ...'

Madame Moreau smiled gently. 'I'm sorry, I had no right to ask that question. Please forgive me. I spoke out of turn mainly because you're the first girl he has ever brought home. The others he would never invite; when I suggested he brought them home, he'd just smile and say that they were not important. Now do you see why I've asked you?'

Felicity moistened dry lips. 'Yes, but I'm not sure. Curt is so overwhelming, so dynamic, too much a man.'

'And would you have him less a man?'

Madame Moreau looked intently at the delicate features suffused pink with embarrassment and uncertainty, and her eyes lingered on the golden hair forming a halo about the small head against the background of the window.

Felicity's voice was more firm. 'No, I don't suppose I would, but there's this feeling of being rushed into something—something that will take me away from everything I love and have become used to.'

'And don't you think Curt isn't aware of it? I've brought up my son with a rigid sense of right and wrong, but I haven't spoiled him with a maudlin love. My own marriage was wonderfully happy and I allowed my husband to bring up Curt as a man.'

'I can see that when I compare him with my brother Blain, who's been hopelessly spoiled by my mother.'

Madame Moreau shook her head. 'We all have a great deal to learn from life, and the young especially. Not all mothers conform to being sensible over their sons. But I've taught my son that love is the most important thing in life, and that the wealthiest people are mere paupers if they have never known it or practised it.'

'He's very arrogant and self-sufficient.'

'Pouf!' Madame Moreau snapped her fingers. 'And what man worthy of the name is not a little arrogant, my dear?'

Felicity gave a nervous little laugh. 'You sound awfully eager for me to marry Curt.'

'I am. I know you can make my son ideally happy; you are a very sweet, very feminine and understanding person. Curt needs a wife and children of his own to learn first hand of human frailties. He was a brilliant boy at school and he's a very clever lawyer. He has an excellent career at his fingertips because he's strong-minded.' The older woman smiled rather wistfully. 'Before his father died, Curt was easy-going and didn't take life too seriously; now he can be ruthless and very scrupulous.'

Felicity smiled. 'You're a dear, Madame Moreau, for telling me about Curt. But I'm afraid he has already charmed me into submission. I have no idea how long I can hold out against him.'

'Don't,' said Madame Moreau, adding as she turned towards the door with the swift graceful movement habitual to her, 'Come down when you're ready. I put dinner off until you both arrived.'

CHAPTER FIVE

THAT weekend in Paris was a wonderful one for Felicity. With Curt still managing to look carelessly elegant in sports shirt and slacks, they roamed the famous parts of the city, stopping here and there for an iced beer or coffee at one of the open-air cafés, to watch the motley crowds drifting by. It pleased her to see Curt relax and shed the taut vitality habitual to him. They shared laughter and a complete and absorbing interest in the same things, and each time his smile flashed out her heart did crazy things.

They had Saturday lunch beneath the centuries-old beams of an enchanting eating-place in the Latin quarter— creamed vegetable soup, a featherlight pancake of ham covered in a delicious sauce, tender steaks with mixed vegetables, pineapples in Kirsch, a bottle of burgundy and coffee. Later they strolled past the artists at work in the quaint main square of Montmartre and went on to enjoy the splendour of the Louvre.

Madame Moreau, busily engaged in her own social activities, left them alone to their own devices, but Curt insisted that she went out to dinner with them on Saturday evening. Curt was an excellent guide and companion, and Felicity, lost beneath the spell of his casual charm, his strength and vitality, his careless fingers on her elbow, longed to clasp his hand and hold it closely.

But although he could not have been more considerate in his bantering, easy way, he never kissed her or embraced her again. He was generous to a degree, and when he purchased a bottle of his mother's favourite perfume by Jean-Marie Farina, he bought her the same and a beautiful three-stringed necklace of perfectly matched pearls. Paris abounded with lovers, arms entwined, and Curt smiled down at her mockingly when they happened to pass a particularly demonstrative couple standing locked in each other's arms.

It was during that weekend in Paris that Felicity began to realize that her former life, happy though it had been, had not been complete. She knew now that there was a greater companionship than that of a brother. She was deliriously happy in the knowledge that love was the essential part of every woman's life, that the love of a man who would protect her and make her feel wanted.

It was a new and thrilling sensation to find herself taken care of in a way which Blain, who had always been too busy thinking of himself, had never done. They returned to London on Sunday night, and when Curt delivered her to her door and drove away, Felicity knew that she loved him desperately. She wanted him with her for all time, and her home meant nothing, so great was her need of him. Her life was empty now he had gone, and it was with a great effort she pulled herself together, telling herself he would come back.

The next week was the longest she had ever lived through. There was no word from Curt, but the roses arrived each day with his card. Several times she lifted the telephone to call him, but pride always made her put it down. Blain came home the following weekend. They went riding together, played tennis and dined out with friends, with Felicity feeling more like an onlooker than an actual participant.

With a sense of shock Felicity realized that although her love for Blain was still as deep as ever, their close association through the years was now less important; the tie between them was becoming less strong. She was fearful of leaving the house in case Curt rang up.

Blain was going back to his regiment on Sunday night and they were having a last drink together after dinner. Her brother, lounging comfortably in his chair, picked up the drink at his elbow and said, 'I saw our friend Curt Moreau two evenings this week. Guess who he was dining with?'

Felicity shook her head. 'You tell me,' she answered with a lightness she did not feel.

Blain found it necessary to take a long pull at his drink before he answered.

'Nora Staffordly,' he said at last. 'You know, I suppose, that they're very old friends?'

Felicity stared down into the drink taken merely to keep her brother company. Miserably, she was beginning to understand Curt's former constraint during the weekend in Paris. It had been he who had set the pattern of their behaviour, he who had been keen-eyed about her wants and endeavoured to keep her happy. How clever he had been to keep within the limits of platonic friendship! It had been entirely by accident that they had discovered their fondness for the same kind of music, beautiful old buildings and works of art. The harmony of togetherness in which she had revelled had not been the spontaneous recognition of twin souls made for each other, it had been the brain child of Curt. But why?

The lovely memory of that weekend was gone. Their friendship rushing headily to the promise of love's fulfilment, the shared fun and laughter which she had hugged jealously to herself, had been a figment of her imagination. Curt's lean brown features swam before her eyes. Those long brown fingers which she had begun to know so well would never caress her. They were reserved for women more experienced and exciting than herself. He might have even found her rather naïve and amusing, a refreshing though rather dull change from the kind of women he knew. She almost cringed at the thought and in that moment hated Nora Staffordly and her kind with a fierce hate entirely alien to her sweet nature.

With a great effort she managed to keep her voice steady although her lips felt stiff and cold.

'She's a client of his, Blain. Don't forget you're in it together. You and . . . Nora Staffordly.'

'Hell! Don't I know it,' Blain answered with brotherly candour, 'I can't sleep for thinking about it. I wish it was all over.'

'You can't wish it more than I,' Felicity answered, wondering how one set about falling out of love. Then, like the warm-hearted, unselfish person she was, she leaned forward and patted his hand. 'Don't worry, Curt is very clever. He'll get you out of it if anyone can.'

'Of course he will, darling.'

Elvira came into the room having overheard the last remark, and perched herself on the arm of her son's chair. Ruffling his curls fondly, she glanced at the exquisite diamond and platinum watch on her wrist.

'You're cutting it fine, Blain, it's time you were off,' she reminded him.

He drained his glass and said irritably, 'Don't fuss, Mother. I've plenty of time.'

Elvira smiled placatingly. 'Now you know, darling, how I hate the thought of you speeding back to London. Be a good boy and give yourself plenty of time.'

'Oh, all right.' Blain put down his empty glass and rose grudgingly to his feet. 'Anyone would think you wanted to be rid of me. Speeding to London might be good practice; who knows, I might take up motor racing if the worst comes to the worst.'

Elvira's face paled at the thought. 'Oh no, darling! Anything but that!' she cried.

But Blain only laughed, and, kissing his mother, flicked a careless hand in Felicity's direction and went out to his car.

'He's only teasing, Mother. Don't look so stricken. It takes money to go in for motor racing, and you provide most of that. Blain couldn't do it on the allowance he gets from Daddy,' Felicity said consolingly. 'You can always refuse to give him the money.'

Elvira looked thoughtful. 'So I can. Thank you, Felicity, you're a sweet child. I wish Blain were more like you in his ways.'

She smiled faintly, as Felicity had meant her to, and left the room.

By ten o'clock, Felicity was in bed staring into the darkness, hard-eyed. In Paris there had been moments when she had been hard put to it not to wind her arms around Curt's neck and draw down his dark head for her kiss. And in such romantic surroundings Curt might have succumbed, even to telling her of a love he did not feel. The only consolation was that he would never know how her bones melted at his nearness, and how even the memory of him filled her with an aching longing.

To be fair, he had not deceived her in any way. She had only herself to blame. Now she had to forget, and try to pick up the pieces to start again. But she couldn't settle to anything indoors and her heart lurched painfully each time the telephone rang. So when David Colston rang her up on Monday afternoon to ask her to go out to dinner with him, she accepted.

She went out every evening that week, dancing at the parties of friends and playing tennis in strenuous matches at the local tennis club in order to take her mind off Curt. The roses still arrived every day, and she could only think that he had forgotten to cancel the order.

'Mr. Moreau busy?' Anna asked on Thursday, as Felicity prepared for an evening out at a birthday ball of a friend.

Felicity smiled briefly. 'Very,' she replied with grim candour.

'The roses are lovely. Must cost him a pretty penny,' remarked Anna sagely. 'They say absence makes the heart grow fonder.'

Felicity grimaced. 'There's always the telephone. And

don't tell me he has laryngitis.'

The other's eyes softened. 'Do you want him? That's the point.'

'I don't know for sure,' she answered slowly, adding whimsically, 'that's the trouble.'

Anna looked at her critically. 'The trouble with you is you don't recognise a real man when you see one. Curt Moreau will still be a dish at seventy. And one is never too old to appreciate amusement and happiness, both of which he'll provide even at that age.'

Felicity did not reply. She rose from her seat at the dressing table and put out her hand for the evening wrap Anna was holding. Her smile was briefly mocking, and Anna, seeing the shadows in her deep blue eyes, put a strong, friendly arm around her shoulders with the wrap. 'Why not accept what fate has to offer? The Curt Moreaus don't come very often.'

At the ball Felicity did not miss a dance. Popular as always among her friends, she laughed and flitted from partner to partner with all her old vigour. It was at the end of the evening when she was being taken home that all the life went out of her.

Her escort, a fellow officer of Blain's in the Guards, had hopefully offered to escort her home.

At her door, he said boyishly, 'There's a dance at the officers' mess this weekend. I'd deem it an honour if you'd come with me.'

She shook her head. 'Some other time, perhaps,' she murmured, and went indoors swiftly. Before long she was creeping into the illimitable comfort which a soft bed brings to weary limbs.

A note came with the roses the following morning. Curt had written without preliminary. 'Picking you up at two' was scrawled in his masculine hand on the card.

'Who does he think he is?' Felicity cried. 'For all he knows I could have made arrangements to go out this afternoon.'

Anna looked at her indignant face and smiled at the rose colour flooding into her pale cheeks.

'I think the blue dress, don't you?' she suggested with a twinkle.

Curt stood waiting by his car when she appeared. He was smoking a cigarette, his profile clear-cut against the sky as he exhaled and stared thoughtfully across the garden. There was a leashed vitality about him, in his firm, determined stance, almost Latin in his entire concentration of thought, sent her heart thudding against her ribs. Then he turned, saw her, and quickly ground out the cigarette with his heel. He was perfectly at ease, as if it was perfectly all right to meet her again after a week's silence which needed no explanation. He showed not the least embarrassment and Felicity was torn between wanting to hit him and throw herself into his arms.

'Where are we going?' asked Felicity in a low voice directly Norton Towers was left behind.

'To the Garden of Eden,' came the answer.

Her heart suddenly accelerated at the look in his eyes.

'Tell me more,' she murmured.

'You'll know in due course,' he answered laconically.

They arrived early at Glyndebourne, and all at once she knew that it was to be the most important date of her life. It was a breathless summer afternoon and the midges were out in force around the lake, but she was only conscious of the man moving with graceful nonchalance by her side. His light grip on her elbow was setting inward fires burning fiercely.

'A perfect setting, wouldn't you agree?' he said, his voice strangely deep.

She nodded and he went on, 'I've been looking forward to this all week. I've had a devil of a time, and I haven't been able to call my life my own. But I have achieved results, and I have a feeling this is my lucky week.'

Felicity did not ask him what he meant, she was too bemused. The air around the lake was cool, the glades heavenly and the velvet green lawns gave a sweet earthy scent which mingled with the flowers. It was impossible not to enjoy an opera in such heavenly surroundings.

They sat silent through the first act, lost in the music and the superb acting and singing.

'Did you enjoy it?' he asked, as he seated her at their little table for supper on the lawn.

'Very much.'

They had finished their meal when he reached for her hands across the table.

'I refuse to go through another week like this one,' he told her with masculine determination, his eyes holding her own captive by sheer strength of will. 'You have to marry me, and soon.'

The rustle of silk accompanied by a subtle perfume swept up to their table and before Felicity had really taken in his words a voice spoke somewhere behind her head.

'Curt! What a lovely surprise! You didn't say you were coming here when I saw you last evening. You naughty boy!'

Felicity sat very still as Nora Staffordly swept up to confront them both. Her smile, which included them both, lingered on Curt's dark face.

Slowly he rose to his feet, gave a mocking little bow and said, 'Well met, Nora. You're the first to know—I've just proposed to Felicity. She hasn't given me her answer yet, but I refuse to take no, so she had better be warned.'

He sat down again, but the look of a lover smouldering in his eyes hardly registered on Felicity's consciousness. She was looking at Nora Staffordly and thinking that she had never seen her looking so lovely. Her white skin, her gleaming red hair, her gold dress shimmering like molten metal in the rays of the evening sun, were breathtaking. If she had been dealt a mortal blow, and Felicity felt that she had, she betrayed no sign of it. For a moment a flash, so faint that it scarcely touched the white skin, warmed her cheeks. Then with a gesture of infinite grace she held out her hand to Felicity, who affected not to see it. The hand was dropped and this time the colour flooded Nora Staffordly's face at the direct snub.

A hard look came into the amber eyes and the tired look about her lids became more discernible. Stiffly erect she said, 'Congratulations, Miss Vale-Norton, Curt. I must return to my friends. It will soon be time for the second act.'

Mrs Staffordly had not spoken a moment too soon, for Felicity was aware of Curt rising to his feet to take her arm and escort her back into the opera house. The second act was even more wonderful than the first and Curt gave a sigh of satisfaction at the end of it. They went back to their table on the lawn again and he was opening a bottle of champagne.

'Well, Miss Vale-Norton,' he said banteringly as he poured out the bubbling liquid. 'What do you say to our getting married? I might add before you give me your answer that any objection will be strictly overruled.'

He passed her glass and laughed mockingly into her flushed face. She watched him pouring out a second drink for himself, loving the strength of his hands and the interested angle of his arrogantly poised head.

'It seems I have no choice,' she said demurely.

'You have one,' he corrected her, 'you can choose to marry me.'

'Do you always get your way in this dastardly fashion?' she demanded.

'Always,' he said darkly with a mocking grin. 'Here's to us.'

Was it her fancy, or did she hear Nora Staffordly's laugh on the still night air? Whether she had or not, the sound echoed in her brain as Curt leaned forward across the table after putting down his glass.

'What about a kiss to seal the bargain?'

With the laugh ringing in her ears, Felicity said stiffly, 'This is hardly the place, is it?'

He looked startled at her set face. 'I'd say there was none better, but have it your way. I can wait.'

His eyes deepened and darkened as they looked into hers and her heart raced, making her breathless. He insisted upon her taking a second glass of the champagne before they left and packed their picnic things together. Then he was manoeuvring his car from the car park, taking the main road and pressing down the accelerator.

Felicity knew he would stop, as he did when they turned off into a quiet road. Deliberately, he slid an arm around her and placed a lean finger beneath her chin. Then he bent his head and her heart did crazy things as his mouth found hers, this time determined to have his way. To Felicity it was like standing close to a furnace, an agony of joy. The heat was there, taking her breath, devouring her until she trembled with a mixture of exhilaration and joy tinged with fear. He was all passion and fire. He represented what life was all about, all that it meant in the fulfilment of womanhood.

When he released her she gasped, and he laughed down into her face before looking suddenly contrite.

'Darling, was I a brute?' he said. 'It's your fault for being so desirable. You even made me forget to give you the ring.'

The next moment it was on her finger, and some of his arrogance went as he asked her anxiously if she liked it.

'It's beautiful,' she breathed, gazing down in awe at the perfect sapphire twinkling happily at her.

'The blue of your eyes,' he whispered, his lips moving down her neck and into the hollow at the base of her throat.

There was a light coming from the tall windows of the library when they returned to Norton Towers.

Felicity, noticing it, remarked, 'Daddy's still up. Mummy and he have been out for the evening.'

'Good,' said Curt, unperturbed, 'I'd like to see him.'

She went with him to the library where the Colonel was in the act of choosing a book to take to bed. He looked up, bushy eyebrows raised, when Curt walked in with an arm around his daughter.

Curt came right to the point. 'Sorry to disturb you at this hour, sir, but I have news for you; I've just asked your daughter to marry me. I hope you approve.'

The older man looked at them both beneath beetling brows. 'I'll have to if she has consented,' was the uncompromising answer. But his look at his favourite child was decidedly humble. Her radiant face told him that he had lost her to a man he admired but did not wholly like. His look was suddenly fierce when he gazed over her head as she flung herself into his arms.

'You have a prize, my boy. Make sure you take care of her, that's all I ask.'

'I'm sorry I'm taking her from you, sir, but I have a bit of news which I'm sure will make you feel better. Staffordly is dropping his suit for divorce. He and his wife are to live in Paris,' Curt told her.

Felicity recalled those words later in her room as she tried vainly to go to sleep. Blain would be on top of the world when he heard about it and she was glad for his sake, even more for her father, who would have found the scandal hard to live with. Why then was she so restless? Being engaged to Curt should send her pie-eyed with happiness. If only Curt had told her about the Staffordlys having second thoughts about the divorce before Nora Staffordly had come to their table at Glyndebourne, in which case she would not have snubbed the woman. She felt so mean about it, but she had been angry with Nora for bringing Blain into her sordid life.

For some reason Nora Staffordly always succeeded in

making her feel uncomfortable. There seemed to be something about her, a tragic aura which reflected in her lovely eyes. Irritably, Felicity asked herself why the woman had to keep intruding into her life; first it was Blain, now Curt. Had it been Curt who had persuaded Staffordly not to go on with the divorce, or was it Nora? But they were questions that her tired brain refused to handle, and she fell asleep at last from sheer exhaustion.

CHAPTER SIX

THE dinner party Elvira gave the following weekend was partly to celebrate her daughter's engagement, and partly to celebrate her son's lucky escape from the scandal of a divorce suit. Blain came home on a weekend leave, congratulating himself inwardly and outwardly congratulating his sister upon her engagement. The party was a huge success, with Curt receiving the good wishes of the other guests with his usual urbane charm.

Felicity loved the way his glance in her direction was both enamoured and proprietorial when Judge Greatman, one of the guests, smiled on them benignly and congratulated him on choosing a lovely and intelligent girl. Curt was staying at Norton Towers over the weekend and Felicity watched him go with her father to the library for a last drink together before going to bed. Then she went upstairs to Blain's room.

Blain came out of the bathroom after having a shave. Dressed in his pyjamas, his fair curls ruffled, he looked like a little boy. He grinned at her.

'Hello,' he said, 'shouldn't you be in bed?'

She closed the door and walked leisurely to his bed where she turned and faced him. 'I want to talk to you,' she told him.

He raised a golden eyebrow and flung himself sprawlingly into the nearest chair. His smile was audacious, and it occurred to her that his recent escape from the consequences of a rather sordid affair had left no mark of regret for his behaviour.

He was openly teasing. 'Come on, smile! What are you looking so serious about? Regretting your engagement already?'

77

She said quietly, 'I'm happy enough for myself, it's you I'm worried about.' She saw the colour rush beneath his freshly-shaved skin and continued, 'I don't believe you know how lucky you've been to get out of a divorce case. In fact, instead of regarding yourself as the guilty party, you've probably been cursing your luck at being found out.'

Seated sideways, with a leg thrown over the arm of his chair, one arm along the back, he grinned at her. 'So what?' he challenged impudently.

Felicity dropped on one knee and caught his hand impetuously. 'Blain,' she pleaded, 'surely you can see that you can't go on in this way, gambling, women and drinking? It just isn't any good. Not for you. You're capable of better things.'

'My dear girl, why so serious? I'm having a good time. But I'm going to miss you.'

His fingers closed over hers and he avoided her anxious gaze. His words were flippantly casual, but there was an underlying quality in his voice which to her sensitive ears veiled emotion.

She felt near to tears. 'I'm going to miss you, too. We've always been so close, that's why I want to be sure I won't worry about you when I've gone. We shall still have good times together; you can come and stay with us and you know you can always depend upon me at any time.'

He gave a twisted smile. 'You always were generous. As generous as Mother. Maybe it will do me good to have less money to go on. I'll be careful in future.'

His words, the fact that he did not understand what she was getting at, touched her heart.

'But don't you see? It isn't a matter of being careful. It's a matter of growing up and facing your responsibilities. You'll have to do it some day. Up to now you've just been playing about, even when you've come home for week-ends.' She smiled at him wistfully. 'You will still come home at weekends, won't you, when I've gone? Mother will be dreadfully hurt if you don't. The parents will miss me because I've always been around, don't rob them of your company too.'

'I'll think about it,' he answered with a grin, and squeezed her hand. 'Don't take on so. I'm a fool, I know, but I enjoy life. If it makes you feel any better I'll give you my word that I'll steer clear of married women in future. How's that?'

Felicity winced inwardly at the caressing note in his voice; a promise given lightly and as lightly forgotten. His eyes held that singular and compelling charm women found irresistible, and a very definite shade of distress drew her brows together. Without being aware of it she drew his well-kept, careless hand to her cheek, wishing that her words would take effect, touch some answering chord in him.

'I love you very much, Blain,' she whispered waveringly. 'I don't ever remember you being cruel to anyone. Don't start now by spending your leaves in some dolly girl's flat instead of coming home to your parents. They love you as much as I do. Never forget that.'

Blain looked a little sheepish. 'I promise to be a good boy,' he said. 'I swear I'll come home on every leave.'

Felicity put up a hand and patted the crisp curls with a sigh.

'If only I could believe you!'

She never remembered the few weeks before her wedding very clearly. Elvira made all the arrangements, went with her to buy her trousseau and fell in with Curt's wishes for an early but not too big wedding. They were to be married in the centuries-old village church where all the Vale-Nortons had married through the years. Curt telephoned Felicity on the eve of their wedding, and the sound of his deep voice sent sleep still further away.

'Hello, my sweet,' he said, 'how are you feeling? Queasy, or thrilled and excited?'

'A bit of all three,' she replied rather breathlessly, as her treacherous heart leapt at the sound of his voice. 'I love you very much.'

'Thanks,' laconically. 'I'll show you how much I love you tomorrow. Sleep well.'

And to her surprise, she did.

The inside of the little church was garlanded with flowers and the smart outfits of the guests when Felicity arrived, slim and exquisite in white. With a trembling hand on her father's arm she walked gracefully down the aisle as the music swelled; then Curt turned his head to capture and hold her gaze with his own.

Moments before her heart had been beating so heavily that she had feared whether she would be able to voice her responses. Now she was lifted above her surroundings by eyes that seemed to reach down into her very soul, taking something from her that would never be hers again. She surrendered completely to wonderful moments from time which once passed would never be regained. The perfume of flowers was all around her, mingling with the wild beating of her heart and the last throbbing notes of the organ as she reached Curt's side. Her responses were sweet and clear and, with the weight of the gold band on her slender finger, Felicity walked with Curt to a new life.

On the plane, as they approached the Greek islands where they were to spend their honeymoon, she had to keep glancing at the big brown man beside her to convince herself that he really was her husband. She viewed his clear-cut profile with pride, knew that the arrogant poise of his well-shaped head was as natural as the expensive suit he wore, and had to make a determined effort to look away. There would always be a part of him locked away from her, regarding his work and life up to when they had met. But no one could have been more considerate. His sheer masculine conquest had not blinded her to the fact that life would not be one long honeymoon, but with Curt it would be a perpetual courtship. She was sure of that.

Looking through her window, Felicity stared down to where sun, air, sea and love were to be hers in the village of dazzling white houses lapped gently on the sandy beaches by the Aegean sea. Dreamily, she gave herself up to the ecstasy of the moment. Everything worthwhile that life had to offer was hers, with Curt.

The rest of the day was a dream underlain by a quivering and fearful anticipation of the approaching night which must follow. She trembled at the intimate thought of him. Her whole being felt on fire at the fear of the unknown, for she had never given herself to a man before. But if terror it was, this delicious sensation melting her bones could only culminate in the fulfilment of love.

When at last the door of their suite shut out the world she began to have qualms. The rooms in one of the finest hotels on the island were luxuriously comfortable, with muted wall lights and the indescribable atmosphere which pervades a honeymoon suite. Curt was still in his dressing-room when Felicity slid in between the scented sheets of the bridal bed, and she was quivering when he entered the room to turn off the lights.

The next moment he was sitting on the bed beside her, taking her cold trembling hands in his warm clasp. His voice was deep and vibrant.

'At this moment I want you more than anything on earth, but I'm not insensitive to the fact that you've had a long and tiring day. There's nothing for you to be scared about. One of the qualities which first attracted me to you was your naturalness, with no false note anywhere. I want you to act naturally with me tonight. Follow the dictates of your own heart. You understand?'

She nodded, her fears melting under the impact of his eyes as he kissed her hands.

He continued, 'While we're on the subject, you might as well know that I'm a perfectly healthy, virile man with the

81

usual normal tendencies which I shall make sure never get out of hand.' He was kissing her now, his lips moving down to her throat. 'Tell me,' he murmured against her lips, 'do you want me to go away for tonight, or shall I stay?'

And Felicity could not resist him. Her mouth sought and met his in a deep kiss. She loved him, belonged to him, and he to her. Everything was perfectly natural and wonderful, and only his touch could work the combination which unlocked her heart. In that simple action of surrender to his masculine demands she gave him her vows all over again, and found the ultimate fulfilment of womanhood. And if his passion did flare, as inevitably it did, beneath it was an immeasurable tenderness and love.

So Felicity began her married life more happy than she had ever been. She was the type that, once committed, gave her all; Curt was her lord and master and she wanted it no other way. The honeymoon was something she remembered all her life. The blood ran strong and invigorating like wine through her veins and she abandoned herself wholly to the joy of living and loving. In the hot sun and breathtaking scenery of the island, she felt an affinity with the Greeks, sharing their passion for life and revelling in the beauty of her own body and the sensual pleasure it brought to Curt. Laughter shone in their eyes and rang in their voices as they dived down in the green translucent depths of the water during their early morning swim. Curt's tan gave him a Latin look against which his teeth gleamed astonishingly white. He looked splendidly alive and amazingly fit, and she was sure there was never a more satisfactory lover anywhere.

So happy was Felicity that his domination of her will passed unnoticed, until one morning after their bathe she appeared at breakfast in primrose slacks.

'You're a tantalizing little devil in those slacks,' he commented, surveying her boyish slimness lazily. 'Now go and take them off and put on a dress. I like you in skirts.'

Felicity walked up against him and said wheedlingly, 'You know you don't mean that.'

Half mockingly, he said, 'Don't I?' The deep quality of his voice never failed to stir her. 'I give you five minutes to take them off and put on a dress. Wear them when you're at home, if you wish, but not here while you're with me.' He laughed, kissed the tip of her nose and added, 'Scram!'

He was standing waiting for her when she returned wearing a white linen skirt of box pleats with the same top.

'That's better.' He smiled at her long slim golden legs. 'Come here.'

She went and put her arms around his neck. 'I can see I shall have to take care of my wedding ring, or you'll be putting me in irons,' she murmured against his chest.

He reached up to clasp her wrists and pull down her arms to fasten a gold bracelet on her slender arm.

'Another crack like that and I'll spank you,' he threatened. 'We happen to be going somewhere important this morning, and I prefer you to look like my wife, not some slim boy.'

Curt kissed the tip of her nose and seated her at the breakfast table on the sunny balcony of their suite of rooms. Then, taking the chair opposite to her, he shook out his table napkin and grinned at her questioning look. He explained,

'It's customary for the Mayor here to invite honeymooners to his parlour, to present them with a certificate making them members of the Seventh Heaven Club. This entitles them to "Love, fun, laughter, happiness, friends, hope and peace".' He picked up his fruit juice. 'Cheers, my sweet. In case you don't know it the Greeks call this island the Bride of the Sun.'

The Mayor was a short thickset man in his middle forties, still darkly good-looking and noticeably gallant. He introduced himself, and with a twinkle in his eye performed the short ceremony of handing over the certificate with all the lightheartedness the occasion merited.

'Wasn't he sweet, Curt?' Felicity said later when they were enjoying an iced drink at a quaint little café.

Curt said dryly, 'Apparently he thought the same about you. He looked at you long enough.'

Felicity laughed. 'It was your fault—you would insist upon me being feminine in a skirt. In any case, I thought it was a beautiful gesture on the part of the island to present us with the good wishes on the certificate.'

'Agreed. But I already have them, thanks to you. You're the most captivating piece I've ever known.'

Felicity's heart gave a curious lurch. 'Thanks,' she said, her eyes dancing with amusement.

He laughed with her, and leaned forward. 'There'll be other things I shall want later, such as children. Agreed?'

His voice had become dangerously attractive, and her eyes fell from his as she nodded. A wave of colour swept over her, making her very conscious of herself and him.

He went on with a mocking delight at her confusion, 'No doubt you've noticed that I'm a light sleeper, but no twin beds when we set up our own home. Togetherness is essential for a marriage to survive, and ours is going to do just that. I need hardly say that any objection will be completely overruled.'

Felicity looked up at him then with a haunting smile, half sad, half gay, with a tantalizing dimple denting a curve in her cheek. His eyes caught and held hers as if they would never let them go. They held an imperious demand and something inspiring and passionate passed between them as they sat oblivious to everything around them.

'You're a brute,' said Felicity, 'but I love you and wouldn't have you any other way.'

He chuckled. 'Thanks. You and I must get together some time. What about tonight?'

He threw back his head and laughed outright at the rich colour flooding beneath her skin.

'There was never any doubt of that,' was the demure answer.

Felicity learned a lot about her husband during her honeymoon. He was generous to a fault, heaping gifts upon her, hiring the best horses because he knew she enjoyed riding, and dancing with her until the small hours although he had admitted to not being too keen on the latter.

She loved the covert twinkle in his eyes, his congenital courtesy, his unfailing good manners and his nonchalant approach to life, which along with his other qualities she found most endearing. Felicity refused to think beyond the honeymoon, although she knew it had to end and she had to face banalities. With passionate intensity every precious moment of every precious day was lived to the full. She gave him all her love and passion, and gloried in the giving, through the wonderful sacrament of marriage. In studying him she knew what he wanted, and her mood was his mood.

For the first time in her life Felicity was passionately grateful for the beauty of her face and form, knowing she could satisfy Curt visually as well as physically. Curt was too intelligent to suffer fools gladly and she took good care not to bore him by being playfully naïve. Her native intelligence and wit told her that the best of men were selfish, and that Curt was the kind of man who took what he wanted. But he had an inborn sense of decency and could discipline himself if he wanted to.

They shared long silences together beneath the vast blue sky, and she became his friend as well as his lover in the truest sense of the word. Marriage to Curt had revealed a passion in her which she had not been aware of—a deep primitive feeling leaving her vulnerable to hurt. That he might hurt her some day made her gallant spirit vow that when that day came she would endure it with dignity.

So Felicity began to work on her marriage, treating it like a career, laying the foundations of love and trust wisely—vowing never to bore him and to keep his illusions about her intact, so that no other woman in his life would ever measure up to her standards.

Anna did not ask if she was happy, neither did her parents. It showed in her glowing face and dancing eyes when she went to visit them on her return from her honeymoon.

'So the colt has been broken in,' said Anna as she packed Felicity's favourite things to take back with her to Curt's chambers at Lincolns Inn. 'Men like a girl with spirit, so don't forget to nip him once in a while,' she added wisely to the evening dress she was folding between layers of tissue paper.

Felicity laughed. 'I won't. Half the fun of quarrelling is the making up afterwards, and Curt does it beautifully.'

'I'm sure he does,' Anna commented dryly, 'and don't choke me!'

Felicity was hugging her exuberantly around her neck. 'Oh, Anna, I wish you were married. You don't know what you're missing.'

To which Anna replied darkly, 'What you never have you never miss.' Then she smiled. 'I hope all your troubles are little ones.'

Felicity laughed with pure joy. 'Let us find a house first, please,' she cried.

They found the house they wanted after months of searching, a low creeper-clad, stone-built country house a few miles from Norton Towers on the other side of the village. A grove of trees, half-circling it, acted as a shelter from the winds. Behind the house were the paddocks and orchards with stretches of velvet green lawns stretching away from the terrace and French windows. Curt and Felicity loved Cherry Trees on sight, and they had fun going in search of furnishings for their new home. They both agreed on a simplicity of design and colour which forbade the sin of overcrowding to be their theme. So Cherry Trees gradually became an enchanted place, with a few choice pieces of furniture from her parents and several good paintings and etchings contributed by Madame Moreau.

Curt, amazed at his wife's intelligence and charm, watched her develop enchantingly. In his opinion she had much to learn about life and there was a good deal he could teach her; but he resolved to do so with a sense of humour, a quality that helped him over most difficulties.

He had decided to keep on his chambers at Lincolns Inn, but his man, Henri, was to come to live at Cherry Trees. He proved invaluable in putting up extra shelves and contacting workmen about alterations and repairs. He was also an excellent cook and willingly showed Felicity her husband's favourite dishes.

With her days so full, Norton Towers faded into the background of her life and her visits home were rare. She had a housewarming party to which her parents and Madame Moreau were invited, but Blain was unable to come because his regiment had been posted to Ireland for a short training session. Curt's mother stayed on for a few days, and everything went off happily.

Felicity was a charming and natural hostess, but their entertainment was limited for the first few weeks, as Curt had a mountain of work to catch up with since coming back from their honeymoon. He was away in London during the day, but came home in time to dine in the evening; sometimes Felicity motored down to London to go to a show and dine with him. On these occasions he washed and changed at his chambers in Lincolns Inn.

They had been married a few months when Felicity met him at his chambers, from where they had planned to attend one of Judge Greatman's parties. The evening was very enjoyable and after dinner Curt and Felicity strolled into the small garden for air. The house, as usual, was crowded, and it was a relief to seek the sanctuary of the little garden and listen to the muted sound of London traffic not far away.

They sat on the terrace and looked down on other guests standing in groups talking below. Curt had just settled himself when Judge Greatman strolled out to ask him to spare him five minutes in his study.

Curt's, 'Shan't be long, darling,' rang in Felicity's ears as she stifled a sigh. She was beginning to wonder if being a famous Q.C.'s wife was just as frustrating as being a doctor's. Curt always seemed to be involved with some case or other; there were so many demands upon his time. Leaning back against the cushions of the chair, Felicity closed her eyes and felt a little ashamed at such thoughts. She was wonderfully happy, and she was more in love with her husband now than when they were married, if that were possible.

Cigar smoke drifted upwards to where she sat, followed by the sound of stentorian laughter, and she leaned forward to see two men directly below her standing enjoying a smoke and a chat. Their conversation passed unheeded until one of them mentioned Mrs Staffordly.

'He's opted out, and I don't blame him,' the first man remarked, and rather amused, Felicity wondered who had opted out.

'Has he?' The second man sounded mildly surprised.

'No doubt about that, old man,' said the first speaker. 'Nora has had her wings clipped; Staffordly is beginning to sit up and take notice. Not that I care for him. Never did—supercilious devil.' There was the scrape of a match as the first man lighted a pipe. 'Her affair with young Vale-Norton brought matters to a head.'

Felicity caught her breath and gripped the arms of her chair as the voice went on.

'They're living in Paris—I wouldn't be surprised if Curt Moreau had something to do with Nora going back to her husband. We all know that Nora will do anything for Curt.'

The other man gave an unpleasant laugh. 'Ironical that he should marry young Vale-Norton's sister. A fetching

88

wench—made all the other women here tonight look jaded, I thought.'

His companion agreed. 'Lovely girl. I wonder if she knows about her husband and Nora? I saw Moreau having lunch with her last week, and him hardly back from his honeymoon.'

'Ah well, it takes all sorts. . . .'

The rest of their conversation drifted into the still night air as they strolled back indoors.

Felicity sat rigid. Every word had been a well-aimed stab to her heart, and she shrank back quivering as from a mortal blow. She did not doubt for a moment the truth of what she had overheard. Dazed and sickened by it, for the shame was hers as well as Curt's, Felicity saw her marriage in ruins. She saw Curt as he really was, stripped of all his charm and glamour, and the disillusionment of it showed in her white face and smouldering blue eyes.

It seemed to her that she had awakened from a dream into cold reality. A lifetime of emotion had been packed into the last ten minutes of time. She felt sick and ill, and when Curt returned he was immediately concerned by her pallor.

'Darling, are you ill?' he asked, bending over her with a worried frown and taking her cold hands in his warm clasp.

'Take me home,' she said.

In the car on their way home he kept glancing at her as she lay back in her seat with closed eyes, and she made no demur when he swept her up into his arms upon reaching the house to carry her to their room. It was while she was being borne in his arms up the stairs that Felicity knew the magic still worked, and the effect of his nearness was as shattering as ever. She loved him despite what he had done and, to her everlasting shame, even her pride did not matter. All her vitality and resilience came to the fore. She would not give him up, would not let him know what she had heard.

As he laid her down gently upon the bed, she gave a tremulous smile.

'I'm all right now,' she assured him.

He stood looking down at her anxiously, not entirely convinced.

'I'm going to send for the doctor,' he said, scanning her face.

'No, don't. Please, Curt, I'm perfectly all right.'

He hesitated. 'Very well. I'm going to fetch you some brandy.'

The brandy set her back on an even keel. Curt sat on the bed watching her drink it, his expression still anxious.

'Come to bed,' she said. 'I want you with me.'

That evening taught Felicity a lot; that the past was never wholly past, but was always there to taunt or to comfort. For her own peace of mind her marriage had to work, and sometimes things had to be accepted as they were and not as one wanted them to be. A very determined effort had to be made to put everything she had heard that evening in the background of her thoughts, for to act upon it and demand an explanation from Curt would be disastrous. She had to trust him.

To leave him now, after all they had been to each other, would be like dying. That night she drowned in the sweetness of his embrace in a deep yet agonizing joy. Mindful of her not feeling well, Curt was very gentle with her until her passionate response awoke an answering passion in him. Never, she vowed, would she ever give him cause to go to another woman.

Several days later, when Curt had gone to his work in London, Elvira telephoned to say the Colonel had suffered a slight seizure during the night. The doctor had been summoned but had assured her there was nothing to worry about. He was calling again at midday.

Felicity drove over right away, and her mother met her in the hall.

'He's sleeping, but he's breathing naturally,' she assured her, and her gaze narrowed at the shadows beneath her daughter's eyes. 'You look a bit peaky yourself.'

Felicity, who had felt queasy all morning, smiled gallantly. 'Nothing wrong with me,' she said brightly.

The next moment she had passed out at her mother's feet. She knew directly she came round what had happened; she was lying on the sofa in the lounge and the doctor was standing over her, his hand on her pulse.

'You're going to have a baby, Mrs Moreau,' he told her. 'Fortunately I was coming in at the door behind you when you fell, so I carried you in here. You probably won't have any more trouble. You're healthy enough—all the Vale-Nortons are healthy stock.' He smiled at Elvira, who was standing by. 'The news that the Colonel will soon be a grandfather will be as good as a bottle of medicine for him!'

Felicity went upstairs to see her father when the doctor had gone. He lay very still, and the face he turned towards her as she closed the door and walked to his bed was pale and drawn.

'Felicity, my dear,' he said faintly, and smiled. 'How nice of you to come. It's really nothing serious.'

She put her arms around him. 'How are you feeling, Daddy?'

'Much better. I'm in no pain, just feel tired. I'll soon be up and about again. I'll have to be, won't I?'

'You mean the baby?' Felicity smiled fondly. 'You'll need all your strength running round after your grandson.'

He nodded, and closed his eyes. She stayed with him quite a while after he had drifted off to sleep, then left the room vowing that she would not neglect to visit him so much in the future.

Curt was delighted about the baby. He treated Felicity like a piece of Dresden china and she laughingly told him that having a baby was quite a natural event.

The Colonel was up and about again within a week, and Felicity went to see him every day. Blain wrote to congratulate her and said he was hoping to be home again soon. With the coming of the baby Felicity settled down to prepare for it, knowing that Curt would be much closer to her with a son to link them. She tried to forget about Nora Staffordly, and came very near to succeeding, until the day she went to London with her mother to do some shopping. Elvira had expressed a wish to attend a show of summer fashions, and they had taken the last two seats at the end of the first row when two women passed with the idea of sitting behind them.

The second woman hesitated in front of them and spoke. 'I'd like to take this opportunity to wish you much happiness, Mrs Moreau,' said Nora Staffordly, smiling down at them both.

She was wearing a black velvet trouser suit with the green scarf knotted at the side of her neck, an excellent foil for her red hair. Feeling very much the *jeune mariée* herself, Felicity saw the woman before her as a *femme fatale*, and not at all as a married woman like herself. But she received her congratulations politely with a little smile.

'Thanks,' she replied. 'We're shopping for baby clothes.'

The words were out before she could prevent them, yet Felicity felt she had to say them, if only to let this beautiful self-possessed woman know that Curt really belonged now to his wife and she to him. For no longer than a second a pained expression clouded Nora Staffordly's lovely eyes; then it was gone, so quickly that Felicity was not sure it had ever been there.

'That's wonderful, I'm so happy for you. I'm sure Curt is delighted. He and I are very old friends,' she said quietly.

There was a sincere note in the lovely voice, striking a chord of sympathy in Felicity, and her smile was much warmer as they parted. Her mother, however, was not so sentimental.

'How embarrassing,' she whispered. 'I don't know how she had the nerve to stop and talk to us after nearly wrecking my boy's life!'

Felicity maintained a discreet silence, and when they left after the show Mrs Staffordly's seat was empty.

The early days of her pregnancy were joyous ones. As she waited for her baby to develop its featureless anonymity, living became a suspended animation and delight. On sunny days her spirits soared to church steeple heights. Knowing that fresh air was essential for a healthy baby, Felicity set off on picnics, taking routes on minor roads in the car at Curt's request. One morning she set off with a picnic lunch packed by the admirable Henri beneath a ceiling of blue sky and balloonlike cumulus clouds; larks sang in the meadows and a changing pattern of light and shade washed over the charming landscape.

There was something so fresh and clean about the countryside, she thought dreamily. It was the ideal place to have a baby. Finding a suitable place to eat her picnic lunch, she stopped the car on a rise and looked down on the valley below where a stream like a line of baby blue ribbon threaded its way through the greenery. Blue for a boy, she told herself happily, and with mounting optimism imagined him riding beside her on his first pony. It had to be a boy, with Curt's exciting dark looks and the same well-shaped arrogant head.

Felicity munched an apple after her lunch and after reading for a while went back to the car, and negotiating the narrow winding road with care, drove on towards Norton Towers. The scent blew across the road from the woods on either side and she could see mists of blue, enchanting bluebells nestling at the feet of thick old trees. The gardens of Norton Towers had all the glamour of the woods, the perfume of flowers and grass and the song of birds as she drove along the gravel to the entrance.

Colonel Vale-Norton was on the terrace, taking his usual afternoon nap after lunch. On his lap was an adorable sealyham puppy who cocked one eye open at Felicity's approach and gave a miniature growl.

The Colonel gave a grunt and opened his eyes at Felicity's chuckle.

'Daddy,' she cried, 'what a poppet! Isn't he sweet? Can I cuddle him?'

She picked up the small white furry bundle, hugged him and gurgled with delight when the small pink tongue licked her cheek. Her father looked a trifle embarrassed.

'Hello there,' he said. 'Had to have something when you went. I call him Whisky.'

'He's adorable,' was her delighted comment. 'But what does Mummy say? She never did like dogs.'

'Your mother is away—went this morning to see Blain in Ireland. Don't know what she has to go for, when the boy's coming home on leave in a week or so.'

Felicity said simply, 'Blain means a lot to her, Daddy. We have to bear with her.' The pup was returned to his lap. 'I don't intend to spoil my son as she's spoiled Blain.' She sat down on one of the white Gothic-style wicker chairs, and smiled fondly at her father. 'He's going to love you.' Her smile was suddenly impish. 'It might be a girl.'

'I'm all for it,' he answered, 'she's sure to be like you.'

She laughed, 'Flatterer! How about coming over for dinner this evening? I'll telephone Curt to collect you on his way home.'

Curt arrived home at seven that evening, having collected the Colonel on the way.

He said with a charming smile, 'Hello, my sweet, I've brought our guest.' Felicity's heart somersaulted at his smile. The magic was still there and she went impulsively into his arms. There was the swift light pressure of his arms, then his mouth covered hers firmly, warmly.

To Felicity the house came to life when Curt was there.

94

The peculiar subtle flavour of his personality was almost tangible as she linked the two most important men in her life indoors. Dinner that evening was a gay meal, with Curt as usual the perfect host, attentive and amusing. He treated the Colonel as he would his own father, and the conversation was shared and enjoyed by all three.

They had coffee in the lounge and the Colonel accepted his cup, looking happily replete with an excellent meal.

'The coffee smells good,' he said with a smile of appreciation as Henri brought in the tray. 'Your man Henri is a treasure. The meal was excellent.'

Curt grinned. 'He's our man now, sir. He's giving Felicity lessons in French cooking.'

The Colonel looked fondly at his daughter. Since expecting her baby she had, in his opinion, an almost *spirituelle* beauty; if only she did not feel things so deeply! He was so afraid of her getting hurt. She was still something of a child with her infallible beliefs in human nature. It had interested him enormously watching her develop, encouraging in her a vivid and stimulating interest in people and in life around her. Since her marriage he had become firm friends with his son-in-law, and appreciated him more than he was inclined to do at the beginning. He could vouch that Curt was one of those rare men who never failed a friend, and on whom it was always possible to rely. But his mind, like his body, was of tempered steel. He was flexible and philosophical, Felicity was neither. She was all deep-down warmth, all heart. However, there was nothing more that a father could tell her. She had to learn by experience, and he hoped it dealt kindly with her. And while he was very happy to see her so content, his smile as he kissed her on leaving was a little sad.

Felicity was thinking about that smile when Curt returned from taking her father home; she had finished her preparations for bed and was already in it, looking very young and vulnerable in her filmy nightdress.

Curt yawned somewhat ostentatiously. 'Ye gods, I'm tired,' he said, beginning to undress.

'Then come to bed, darling,' she said softly, feeling the familiar quickening of her pulses underlying the troubled thoughts of her father. 'Daddy looked a little lost tonight. He's bought the cutest little dog for company. He misses Blain in Ireland, and me. I feel worried about him.'

She studied his face as he came to her and found it more exciting than ever as his arms reached out with a consciousness of mastery. He frowned for a moment at the concern in her deep blue eyes, then did the obvious thing, and that was to close her mouth with kisses. His body, close to hers, hard, muscular and strong, seemed to enfold her with his strength when he spoke at last against her lips.

'Your worries are mine too. I'm your husband, remember? Your father will be all right. Why not ask him to stay with us until your mother returns home?'

That night Felicity dreamed that she was back again at Norton Towers. She was young again with Blain, playing in the woods and dancing with delight because it was spring. They gathered flowers and fern wet with dew and pelted each other with them. Then they played at hide and seek among the trees and Blain was playing hard to find, as he always did. She kept calling his name, but there was only an echo, and she searched and searched until she sank down on the grass, exhausted, to fall asleep. Suddenly she heard his voice. He was bending over her to kiss her gently and she awoke with his name on her lips.

'Steady now. It's all right, my sweet—you've been dreaming.'

Curt drew her into his arms and stroked back the heavy golden hair from her hot forehead.

Felicity looked up at him wide-eyed and distraught. 'Did you kiss me just now?' she asked.

'No. You woke me up yelling "Blain" at the top of your voice. You've been dreaming,' Curt said philosophically.

'Then it was Blain who kissed me. It woke me up. It was almost as though he was here in the room; I heard his chuckle as plain as I can hear you.' Tears rushed to her eyes and her voice trembled. 'Oh, Curt, do you think something dreadful has happened to him?'

'There, you're taking a dream far too seriously. Of course nothing has happened to him. Your mother is there by now with him, remember? Blain is a big boy now, my sweet,' he said gently. 'Forget all about him and go off to sleep. Close your eyes.' He kissed her eyelids softly and she slept.

CHAPTER SEVEN

FELICITY slept late the following morning, and seeing the time knew that Curt had left her sleeping. He left the house at eight-thirty each morning, and it was now nine o'clock. With the morning sun streaming in through the window the disturbing dream of the previous night lost its menace; it was only a dream and her family had been very much on her mind before she had gone to sleep.

She towelled herself vigorously after taking a cold shower and slipped her bare feet into sandals. Her dress, white cotton with embroidery around the square neck and full skirt, was cool and dainty, and she left her hair loose to fall into its own shape as it curled softly around her oval face.

As she dressed, Felicity's thoughts were on her father. I ought, she told herself with compunction, to have asked him to stay last evening instead of letting him go back to Norton Towers with only Anna and the staff to keep him company—no doubt he had expected her to do so. He must have thought me very uncaring, she told herself. If she had been a little thoughtless it was only because of a deep-seated unwillingness to share Curt with anyone. They saw so little of each other, for he was away all day and they were only together in the evenings and weekends. But her family was different. She would drive over at lunch time and bring her father back with her.

'The men have finished work in the nursery, madame,' Henri said when he came to clear away the breakfast dishes. 'They would like you to go and look at it before they leave, in case you want anything altered.'

It was perfect, lovingly planned by herself and Curt. Pale green walls restful for precious eyes; pretty nursery furniture, white with Walt Disney painted motifs of animals and birds; cupboards and shelves built within easy reach for toys. In one corner, still in their wrappings, were a rocking horse from her parents and a teddy bear from Blain.

With eyes rather misty and mouth sweetly curved, Felicity found herself thinking of the old nursery at Norton Towers where she and Blain had played so happily together. Now Blain would soon be an uncle and she would be a mother. She walked across the room to look out on the tree outside the window, a must for a nursery where the baby would see the birds nesting and fussing over their young. Below the garden was fresh and green, full of mystery for a child, drenched in folklore and the promise of fairies.

Lost in her dreams, Felicity swung round, startled, to hear Henri say that she was wanted on the phone.

It was Anna. 'Can you come at once?' she said urgently. 'I think the Colonel has had bad news. A telegram arrived not long ago, and he's sitting in his study. He won't allow me in.'

Felicity's hand was shaking when she put down the telephone. Calm yourself, she told herself firmly, nothing to be gained in getting in a panic. Poor Daddy! She must go right away. The room had darkened suddenly without her noticing it as clouds covered the sun, bringing a swift shower of rain beating down fiercely on the windows. She shivered. It was like an omen of disaster.

Without waiting to collect a coat, she ran from the house to the garage, ignoring the heavy rain spattering her pretty dress and flattening her hair. She had driven half way down the driveway when the car skidded. The tree loomed suddenly in her path; frantically, Felicity forced the wheel round. There was the sudden screeching of brakes followed by broken glass, then blackness.

*   *   *

She came round to the smell of antiseptic and clinically white walls. Dim forms moved all around her and a masculine voice was saying, 'Poor child. Bad enough to lose one baby, but two. . . .'

The words struck her to the heart, deadening all feeling, leaving her with the incredulous bewilderment of a child who had lost its way in the dark. The sound of voices buzzed in her ears, shutting her in. Bright lights dazzled in fantastic shapes with flashes of colour that hurt her eyes. She wanted to scream for them to go away, but she knew her own voice would be drowned by the echo of those cruel words returning again and again. 'Bad enough to lose one baby, but two. . . .' Two babies. Twins. The realization that she had been going to have twins and that she had lost them made her feel physically sick.

Her whole body felt at the mercy of cruel, remorseless hands that were tearing her inside apart, until she wondered how it was possible to endure such agony and live. The heat of the lights seemed to bring them closer until sweat oozed on her temples and she gasped for air. Then, mercifully, the torturing hands had gone and only the voices remained. Why did they have to go on talking? What was it to them? Her babies had meant everything to her and nothing whatever to them. Now her babies had gone and she wanted to get away, anywhere from the constant drone of voices saying meaningless things.

Surely they would let her go away now from the hot, torturing lights, the pain and the smell of antiseptic. Even animals were allowed to go away and lick their wounds. But her wounds were the kind that would not heal; they scarred her mind and thoughts. Felicity often wondered how she managed to survive that ordeal, in what to her was a torture chamber of blinding lights and the continuous drone of voices intent upon one thing—to drive her out of her mind. Then mercifully the voices droned away into one. A tap was turned on and there was a slight rush of air as a door was opened. At last she was out of the room, being borne swiftly along a cool, wide corridor. The relief, the utter sense of peace was overwhelming. Exhausted, Felicity breathed in deeply and slept.

For a week Felicity was allowed no visitors, during which time she lay there like a waxen doll discarded by some careless hand. She was awakened, washed, fed and her bed made, and none of it seemed to be happening to her. She had not the energy to count the days until, one day, she opened her eyes to see Curt sitting beside her. His eyes were dark with anxiety and love.

'My poor sweet,' he murmured, and gathered her gently in his arms.

And it was only then, safe in the haven of his strong arms, that the numbness and horror of all that had happened rose in one tidal wave. She crumpled against his chest into a storm of weeping that shook her to her very soul.

In vain he tried to calm her, but she was past calming herself. The ice around her heart relaxed its hold, the numbness in her brain began to dissolve and she began to feel again things she had tried to forget.

Choked by sobs tearing at her slender frame, her eyes blinded by tears, Felicity clung to him while he stroked her hair and murmured soothingly until the storm that engulfed her gradually abated. It swept away all thought and reason, leaving one quivering and inexorable truth—that the babies she might have had were no more, and the life she had built around them was now no more than a dream. Her desolation and despair were all the more shattering because she alone had been responsible for losing them. If only she had taken more care. Poor Curt! She had done this terrible thing to him as well.

She lifted her head when he passed her his handkerchief, and wiping her eyes, looked up to see something more shattering than grief in the steady composure of his face.

'I'm ... sorry ... Curt,' she stammered, and a passion of tears shook her again as she went on incoherently. 'Do ... say ... you forgive me. It was all my fault.'

She spoke the words against his chest, unable to meet his look in case she saw disillusionment and condemnation in his eyes. He had given her a love and tenderness and a grand passion which in itself had all the fire of vibrant life. With him she had explored all the enchantment and mystery of love which his absolute sympathy and understanding had made the most perfect thing in her life. The babies had gone, but she still had Curt, who meant more to her than anything else in the world.

His voice seemed to come from a distance, soft words of assurance which he whispered in her hair, bringing her ultimate comfort, crushed as she was still by the enormity of her sense of loss. His lips caressed her poor swollen eyelids and he was kissing her almost reverently, tasting the salt of her tears and all her sweetness beneath them. Against the whiteness of her pillow, her pale face, quivering lips and deep blue eyes with the golden hair disordered and curly had never looked so lovely. Now with her arms around his neck, her pale face flushing with colour and stained with tears, she clung to him weakly.

His kisses spoke more plainly than words, telling her that there was nothing to forgive but everything to live for because they were all the world to each other. Contentment and happiness lulled her into a sense of peace. She felt better. Presently she framed his dark face with her hands in a lovely and compassionate gentleness, and was appalled to see it ravaged with weariness.

'Poor Curt,' she murmured. 'Did I do that to you? I was an idiot rushing off as I did; it was all my own fault.'

He said firmly, 'Put it all behind you where it belongs, in the past. It was meant to be, and that's all there is to it.'

She nodded. 'You're right, but don't you remember? I was going to see Daddy. Where is he? What happened, and

102

why hasn't he been to see me?'

His face darkened with a kind of bitter helplessness, and for seconds the memory of some unspeakable experience seemed to hold him rigid.

'Your father is away at the moment. He's all right, you're not to worry about him. He has me too, you know.'

Again she nodded, but her dark blue eyes were scared. 'Does he know I'm here? And my mother and Blain? Do they know too?'

With nerves stretched and quivering, Felicity waited for his answer.

He paused, taking her hand in one of his and feeling for her wrist and the beat of her pulse with the other.

'My poor sweet,' he answered at length, 'you've been very ill, and if you hadn't rushed off as you did and not shut your car door properly, you wouldn't have been here to see anyone. You were flung clear when your car hit the tree.' A spasm of emotion creased his face before he had it under control. 'For heaven's sake, child, don't you realize you nearly killed yourself? You haven't been well enough to receive visitors.'

His voice had thickened and he was frowning savagely. But already Felicity's mind was on Anna's telephone call, and her own urgent need to see her father.

'I can see him now, can't I?' she pleaded.

'If you persist in all this unnecessary anxiety, you'll see no one,' said Curt with measured firmness. 'You must rest today, or you'll be ill again. I was only allowed in to see you because I'm your husband, and if they discover that my visit has in any way upset you there'll be no more visitors for you for the next few days.' He kissed her hand. 'Be a good girl, and be patient. You'll see him in good time. I can assure you he's all right and sends his love.'

Felicity drew her hand away from his and sat up facing him. Her heart beat suffocatingly, and she spoke with great effort.

'There's something wrong, isn't there? Something has happened that you're keeping back from me. Please, Curt, tell me what it is. It won't make me ill again. I'm never ill.'

Curt looked at her—once, twice, then away again. He said carefully, 'I can see that you're going to make yourself ill if I don't do something to convince you.' He made an abrupt gesture as though compelled against his will into action. 'Would it settle your mind if you spoke to your father on the phone? He's away on business.'

She nodded.

'And you'll rest and not ask any more questions about anything until you're better?'

She nodded again.

With that he left the room, and returned with the telephone on a trolley. Dialling a long-distance call, he smiled at her as he waited.

'Hello?' he said. 'Could you put me through to Colonel Vale-Norton, please? Thank you.' Carefully he turned his face away from her clear-eyed gaze. 'Hello, sir, this is Curt. Your spoiled brat of a daughter insists upon talking to you,' teasingly. 'She refuses to take my word that you're all right, so I'm putting her on. Perhaps you'll convince her that there's nothing wrong.'

He handed her the telephone with a smile, and she took it with trembling fingers.

'Hello, Daddy. How are you?' she said. 'Anna said something about a telegram, and thought it was bad news.'

A pause at the other end, then his voice came strong and clear.

'My dear child, we're always having bad news these days, what with one thing and another. I'm sure Curt has put your mind at rest and told you everything is all right. I don't know what I'd do without him.' His voice grew thick. 'The line is very poor at the moment. I hope you can hear me when I say how very sorry I . . . we all are to hear about

104

your sad loss. But if it's any consolation to you, your mother lost her first baby too. I don't know if she ever told you. She would insist upon going out riding when she was pregnant, and got thrown from her horse.'

Felicity said choked, 'Daddy, how sweet of you to tell me. Can I speak to Mummy?'

'She's with Blain. Now be a good girl and concentrate on getting well! I believe Curt has a letter for you from Blain, posted the day after your accident. God bless. Look after yourself, and put Curt on the line. I want a word with him.'

Curt was on the telephone for a few minutes, then he put it down.

'Well,' he said with a smile upon seeing the question in her eyes, 'what is it now?'

Felicity put out her hand. 'You have a letter for me from Blain?'

He drew a postal packet from his pocket. 'Look at it when I've gone,' he said quickly. 'Nurse will be here at any moment now to throw me out.'

The nurse appeared as he spoke as if on cue, and Felicity wound her arms around his neck as he bent his head.

'You're a pet,' she told him, and her lips quivered. 'Please don't worry about me. I won't think about anything, only getting better.' Her clear eyes met his wistfully. 'I'm going to get over it.'

'You will,' he told her confidently. 'You've got me. I hope you'll always remember that.'

'As though I could ever forget it,' said Felicity.

'As I said, I hope not.' He kissed her, straightened and stood looking down at her, then left the room. There was something about the way he went that made her wonder.

She opened Blain's letter when the nurse had gone. Inside the envelope was a small packet containing a pair of earrings, shamrocks picked out in diamonds. They were accompanied by a brief note, Blain fashion—he always did hate writing letters—and they were exquisite, and must have cost quite a sum.

Dear Felicity, he had written. *Came up on the gee-gees, hence the little gift. It should perk you up. Love, Blain.*

How like him, she thought, not to mention losing the babies; instead he had sent a gift to cheer her. Later, when she could talk about it without pain, she would tell him that there had been two babies. He was sure to make some smart comment about it. But not now. The wound was too raw.

Whenever she looked back on her days in that small private ward in the hospital, Felicity always remembered the flowers. They were everywhere in the room, from stately gladioli to a small bunch of wood violets Anna brought one day, along with some of her delectable cooking.

'You're so thin,' she said, 'you want feeding up.'

Curt collected her on the day she was discharged, carried her to the car and from the car into the house. Henri had lunch all prepared and Curt carried her without preamble into the dining room where he set her down into a chair by the table.

'A pleasure to see you back again, madame,' Henri said as he carried in the champagne and ice.

Curt poured. 'A drink, my sweet, to celebrate your homecoming. An aperitif for the special lunch Henri has prepared.'

Curt teased her during the meal, making sure she ate her share of the food Henri had gone to such pains to prepare— paté de foie gras studded with truffles, a tender chicken casserole with mixed vegetables and thick wedges of cara-mel, glazed apple tart in delicate smooth French pastry top-ped with fresh cream. There were cheeses to follow and Henri's excellent coffee.

After lunch, Curt insisted upon her resting, but she pro-tested.

'But I see so little of you, Curt. I want to make the best of this weekend together.'

He had carried her up to their room. 'Only an hour, my

sweet,' he said, laying her on the bed, 'I have some letters to write, then I'm all yours.'

She had washed and changed when he returned an hour later to their room. 'I refuse to be treated as an invalid,' she said, 'I'm perfectly well.'

He had closed the door behind him and stood leaning against it nonchalantly, his eyes narrowing over her slender figure. He looked strange but beautifully casual in slacks and a cream fair-isle sweater, giving his shoulders the wide span of a baseball player.

'Don't remind me,' he warned. 'I haven't been able to sleep without you. Furthermore, there's something about you, my sweet, that makes me want to go all primitive and ravish you.'

Felicity's face was the colour of a wild rose. She had always known that she had an inner power to whip up his passion, and although he was the first man she had ever been intimate with, she knew that the intoxication their bodies held for each other was something rare. Her eyes fell before his, but not until she had witnessed the aching and longing in his.

When he came across the room to her there was only a mocking tenderness in his gaze and the strength to wait.

'Well?' he demanded. 'What do you want to do this afternoon? Your wish is my command. I thought a run in the car to some quiet lake where we can drift along lazily on the water; a light tea somewhere, then an evening at home listening to our favourite music before an early night.'

So that was what they did. When Felicity dressed for dinner that evening she put on Blain's earrings. Curt congratulated her on her appearance, admired the earrings and changed the subject. It was later, when she was in bed and Curt was slipping in beside her, that she said, 'I wrote and thanked Blain for the earrings. I'm sure Daddy said he was due home this week on leave. I suppose Mummy is waiting to come back with him, Daddy too.'

Curt took her gently in his arms. 'No, she isn't,' he said.

'You have to be very brave, my darling. I couldn't tell you before, not until you were strong enough to take the shock, but now I have to.'

'What shock? Curt, what have you been keeping from me?' she cried.

Very slowly, very gently, he told her, 'Your mother and Blain were killed in a car crash on the day your mother went to Ireland to see him.'

She gave a convulsive shudder and his arms tightened around her.

'I'd give anything to spare you this, my sweet,' he went on, his voice rough with emotion, 'but I can't. I can only comfort you.'

Felicity looked at him, blue eyes dilated. His words had left her momentarily speechless.

'You knew, and never told me?' she gasped, trying to take it in.

His expression didn't change. 'I knew.'

She searched his face wildly, as if seeking the lie to his statement.

'You knew all this time,' she said. 'It isn't a long time really, though it seems a long time. And you knew.'

Her voice was a shocked whisper. Her head fell against his chest and she closed her eyes. Presently he stroked her hair soothingly, well in command of the situation. She had not made a scene, for which he was thankful. All the same, he wished she had not clammed up, shutting all emotion inside her.

'You did say dead, Curt? Both of them?' Her voice was hoarse with grief.

'They were both killed instantly. Blain had gone to meet your mother when she arrived at the airport. They left in a car he'd hired, and Blain drove straight at a bollard in the centre of the road. He evidently lost control of the car.'

'But the letter and present he sent! Posted the following day?'

'Posted by his batman. Blain had given it to him to post before setting out to meet your mother.'

'But why? Why should they both die?'

Curt did not answer. Felicity lifted her face, conscious of the powerful curve of his shoulders as his mouth sought and closed on her own with the urgency of a strong man's need long suppressed.

Felicity went to Norton Towers on Monday morning, after Curt had left for the city; she wanted to be there when her father arrived back from Ireland. Curt had told her that he was there to collect Blain's things and to attend the inquest. While one half of her wanted to rush and comfort him, the other half shrank from returning to a home now strangely empty.

The front door had been left open by the thoughtful Anna, and she walked in to the fragrance and peace only to be found in old houses.

'My poor lamb,' said Anna, folding her to her breast. 'As if you haven't enough to contend with!'

'It's Daddy I'm worried about,' admitted Felicity with a pale smile. 'We'll have lunch served in the lounge, Anna, when he arrives. It's his favourite room.'

The lounge was one of the most pleasant rooms in the house, with three tall windows facing south and catching most of the sun. Here there was none of the sombre, dark elegance of the other rooms. The walls were magnolia, hung with gold-framed watercolours, the parquet floor, beautifully polished, was covered in Persian rugs. Deep chairs and a long, low sofa were covered in gay flowered chintz to match the window curtains. Behind latticed windows of corner cupboards were gleaming silver trophies the Colonel had won at polo in his youth, and his mahogany desk with its deep drawers and secret little cubicles was topped by a beautiful crystal vase of his prize roses.

When he arrived Felicity scanned his face anxiously. He

109

looked older and stooped a little as though cringing from the cruel blow fate had dealt him, but he straightened on seeing her and smiled into her look of concern.

'Oh, Daddy!' she cried, and ran into his arms.

'My poor child,' he said. 'Now, no tears. You're not to upset yourself. Come, sit down. It seems you've been through the mill more than I. Was it very bad?'

They walked into the lounge and sat down on the sofa. He took her hand and she tried to curb her emotion.

'Yes, Daddy, it was—I mean, for Curt. He was terribly disappointed, and it was all my fault.'

'I know. You were coming to comfort me. I wish Anna hadn't telephoned you. There was nothing you or I could do about it.' He squeezed her hand as a tear fell. 'Don't worry. There'll be other children.'

Her lips trembled. 'How can I be sure? I might not be able to have any more.'

'Nonsense. We Vale-Nortons are a strong and healthy lot. You might look streamlined and delicate, but then so does a thoroughbred pony. You'll have other children. You and Curt are too healthy to be childless.'

Felicity went from one painful subject to another. 'Tell me about . . . Mother and . . . Blain,' she pleaded.

He released her hand and put his head back against the cushions. Full of compunction for not thinking about it before, Felicity went to pour him a whisky.

'Have something yourself,' he said as she gave it to him.

She poured a sherry, and was coming back to sit beside him when the door opened slightly to allow something small and white to hurl itself across the room and up into the Colonel's arms.

'Steady on, old chap,' he said, putting down his drink to take hold of the wriggling little body as Whisky licked his face frantically in welcome, 'I'd forgotten about you.'

'He hasn't forgotten you,' Felicity smiled as she sat down beside him, thankful that her father had something to keep him company. 'You were saying, Daddy,' she reminded him.

'Oh, yes.' The beetling brows puckered in remembered pain. 'I didn't want your mother to go to see Blain. It wasn't necessary, with him due to come home on leave.' He shook his head absently, fondling the puppy's ears as it lay in his lap. 'He came home all right; they both did, in a box.' He had to take down part of his drink before going on. 'They're in the family vault in the church. It was a very quiet funeral.'

Her eyes misted. 'And I wasn't able to be there with you. I'm so sorry, Daddy.'

'I had Curt. I don't know what I would have done without him. I'll be all right now, of course, with Anna. One thing, though, I hate dining alone. I'll get used to it, I suppose. Could ask one or two of my old cronies in.' His smile was pathetic. 'We live in strange times. Years ago, widows were the fashion. Now it seems that the old order changeth, and widowers are taking over. I'm the fourth in my own circle of friends.'

'But you have Curt and me, Daddy. Would you like to live with us? You'd be very welcome,' she told him wistfully.

'Good lord, no,' was the gallant reply. 'Young people are happier on their own. By the way, I've been thinking things over. I'm thinking of staying at my club in London for a while. There'll be too many echoes in the house yet for me to ignore. Maybe when I return, they'll have gone.'

'Are you sure that's what you want, Daddy?' she asked him quietly.

'That's what I want,' was the emphatic answer. 'There I shan't be badgered with condolences and long faces of commiseration. Not only that, but you can come up to London and lunch with me some days. And there's nothing to stop you and Curt dining with me any evening you feel like it. They always put on a good menu at the club.'

111

CHAPTER EIGHT

FELICITY missed her father during the next few weeks. She made one visit to Norton Towers when he had gone, because Anna wanted to know what to do with Blain's clothes. The gardens were more lovely than ever that summer, but Felicity could not bear to look at them when she arrived. She stood for a long time with Blain's uniform hat in her hands, remembering how he had worn it rakishly on his fair curls. It was hard to believe even now that he was lying still and lifeless, he who had been so full of life. Strange how her mother's possession of him had triumphed even in death.

She had gone with her father to the old church in the village to see the family vault, more precious now since it contained two beloved people. And as Felicity had looked down at the cool harmony of flowers and sunlight filtering through stained glass beneath which they lay, she was soothed and the bitter resentment against a cruel fate that had seen fit to part them gradually disappeared.

Blain's clothes were given away, but his uniform was kept in his wardrobe. Some day, Felicity thought, her son would march about with the uniform hat on his small head and she would tell him all about the uncle he would never see. Elvira's clothes went too, and the room was made solely her father's for when he returned.

Felicity took long walks in the woods and fields around Cherry Trees during her convalescence and the colour gradually returned to her pale cheeks. Her maternity clothes were put away and she shopped for new outfits, lunching in town with Curt on the days that she did so. He was up to his ears in work, and most evenings he was late coming home. He was on a difficult case and during this time he did not return home for three days and slept at his chambers in Lincolns Inn.

Felicity missed him dreadfully, and lived for his telephone calls each night. On the second night he was away the phone rang a little earlier than his usual time for ringing.

'Hello, is that you, Curt?' said a woman's voice.

Taken aback, Felicity replied, 'Curt isn't here. Can I give him a message?'

The reply came quickly, too quickly. 'No, no. It isn't important.'

Putting down the receiver, Felicity knew that the voice had been that of Nora Staffordly. She did not call again, and after her third night without him, Felicity went to lunch with him. Although she had never doubted Curt's faithfulness, Nora Staffordly's dulcet tones on the telephone had filled her with unrest. While she was confident of her husband's love, Felicity had never fooled herself that as a man of great driving force and ability he wouldn't demand far more from life, indeed expect it, than she did. His abundant energy had to have an outlet, and a brilliant career was the only answer.

She had decided while driving up to London not to tell him of Nora Staffordly's phone call, in case he should think she had come to catch him unawares. He had sounded surprised on the telephone when she had called him up this morning, but he had been quite pleasant about it and not in the least put out.

He was waiting for her at the entrance to the restaurant and as he strode forward to greet her, her heart swelled with love and pride at his bronzed fitness and splendid physique. He strode through life with a very decisive vitality stamped on his dark arresting face; it was very easy to imagine the flutter he could cause in other feminine hearts beside her own. Mrs Staffordly's for example.

He had everything arranged even at short notice; he had

booked a table in a corner of the room where they could talk intimately and he had ordered all her favourite dishes. His eyes appraised her smart little cream suit and the wispy hat set deliciously on her fair hair.

He looked at her for a long time. 'Miss me?' he asked.

'So much,' she replied. 'I almost came to your chambers to creep into bed beside you.'

'Why didn't you?' Curt said approvingly, and a charming smile transformed his whole face. 'My poor sweet, I'm afraid I've neglected you shockingly. But today sees the end of my enforced absence.' He leaned across the table, vital and challenging. 'How about coming to court to hear the verdict? I need hardly tell you I'm banking upon winning the case.'

'I couldn't, Curt! Not in a public courtroom,' she gasped.

'And why not?' demanded Curt. Then he grinned. 'Judge Greatman is presiding. He's a wit. You want to hear him, don't you?'

She said simply, 'I want to hear you.'

So she went into the court after lunch and saw Curt in action. He was as sleek as a seal in his black silk, and Felicity decided that the court wig suited his saturnine features, while the breadth of his shoulders beneath the fine cloth made him look, as always, an arresting figure.

Quietly, with every word a punch below the belt, he tore the prosecution's case to ribbons. The verdict was never in doubt. Judge Greatman summed up the case and the jury retired to reach a verdict. Felicity enjoyed the afternoon, since the verdict was the right one of not guilty. She had tea with the Judge and Curt and, after he had changed, they made for home.

'How would you like to go to Paris for a while?' They were on a stretch of road with very little traffic, and Curt tossed her a questioning glance.

Felicity was some seconds collecting her thoughts. It was

a dreamy sort of evening, and the fact that Curt was coming home again had filled her with a blissful content.

'You mean for a holiday?' she asked.

'No. I've been asked to take on a case in Paris, and if I consent it will mean leaving you at Cherry Trees alone. I won't take it unless you want me to.'

The question had put Felicity slightly off her stroke. 'Why ask me, since I know nothing about it? Is it very important to you?'

'Actually it's an honour to be asked to take it on, since there are admirable advocates in Paris who could do the job just as well.'

Felicity looked down at her wedding ring gleaming softly against the slim white hand and kept her head obstinately lowered so that he could not see her face.

'Then it is important to you, isn't it? You'd better go.'

The words were forced from her lips, almost choking her. Her eyes were filled with tears, but her voice remained steady.

'Do I go with your blessing?' he asked mockingly, and she tried to harden herself against the very attractive quality in his voice, never so lethal as when he teased her.

'How long will you be gone?' The inevitable question which left her on tenterhooks waiting for his answer.

'About six months,' laconically.

Felicity did not answer, and Curt drove for a while in silence. Then suddenly he drove the car into a layby at the side of the road, shut off the engine and, with masterful deliberation, laid his hands on her shoulders, turning her until she faced him. Her eyes were still lowered, her wet lashes dark against the paleness of her face.

'Felicity. Look at me,' he commanded, and waited while she slowly raised eyes drowned in tears.

'Your eyes are like drenched violets,' he said. 'Poor sweet, I'm a beast. Does my going away mean so much to you?'

She did not answer.

He repeated the last question insistently, demandingly, twisting the knife in the wound.

'Go on,' he ordered her. 'Does it hurt for me to leave you? because it's hell for me to leave you.'

'Oh, Curt, you idiot,' she said at last on a broken laugh. 'It's like dying. Why did you have to ask?'

'Because I wanted to hear you admit it,' he answered, hauling her fast against him and crushing his mouth on her quivering one.

Felicity gave a helpless gasp and clung to the curve of his wide shoulders with the strength of despair. She was panting for breath when he let her go and she put her hands against him, holding him away.

'When ... are ... you leaving?' she said dully.

'When are we leaving,' he corrected her.

'You mean ... both of us? Shan't I be in the way?'

'No, you will not.'

'But I can't leave Daddy that long,' she told him piteously. 'He's all I have now.'

'Your father left you, remember? He's at his club and enjoying it too. We're dining with him this evening to set your mind at rest.'

The Colonel looked much better when they met him that evening at his club. He said with a twinkle, 'I'm enjoying myself with old cronies, talking over old times. I shall probably stay here during the summer, and go back to Norton Towers before the London fogs.' Then he smiled on them both paternally. 'So you're off to Paris! Well, it's a city for the young.'

'The young in heart, sir,' Curt corrected him with a twinkle. 'I wish you would go for a visit. My mother would be delighted to have you.'

The Colonel nodded. 'A delightful woman, your mother. You must thank her for being so good to my little girl.' He smiled fondly at Felicity. 'Have a good time, my dear, and

116

don't worry about me. I shall be all right.'

'Daddy's right about your mother, Curt,' Felicity said when they were on their way back to Cherry Trees. 'She wrote me beautiful letters after I'd lost the babies—which reminds me, I didn't know you had a brother.'

'Did Mother tell you?' he asked unemotionally.

'Yes. She said he was her firstborn, and he was five years older than you. What was he like?'

'Like Mother,' he answered. 'He liked city life.'

He said no more, and there was that in his voice forbidding further questioning. Felicity felt his sudden withdrawal like a blast of cold air, a small shadow over the brightness of the day. She had reminded him of the past about which he no longer wanted to know, and she moved her slim shoulders as though to shrug off the curiosity burning inside her as to why he should be so offhand about a beloved brother. What did it matter in any case? She was going to Paris with Curt on a second honeymoon.

Still drowning in a pool of bliss, Felicity undressed and got into bed. Presently the vibrant warmth of Curt's lips was at her temple, and she closed her eyes in the heaven of his embrace. Suddenly the sense of depression against fate for robbing her of two beloved people and her babies, which had seized her waking hours, fell away from her in the ecstasy of belonging to Curt.

'What a heavenly villa!' cried Felicity, looking round a spacious room of white and gold built-in furniture, leading into a bathroom of shell pink marble with a sunken bath.

'Like it?' Curt asked from the doorway, leaning against the doorpost, hands deep in pockets, a mocking smile in his eyes.

'Like it?' she echoed on a gurgle of delight as she threw her hat down on to a chair and patted the neat golden fold of hair at the back of her head with a gesture he knew so well. 'It's fabulous! All this light, air and space, and these lovely flowers.'

She looked up at him with sparkling eyes as he strode lazily across the deep carpet to gaze down into her enchanting face.

'Come and see the view,' he said, drawing her out on to the balcony.

Below them the sunken Italian garden was bathed in the golden glow of the evening sun, wisps of pink clouds drifted in an azure sky and were mirrored in the lake fringed by trees. Felicity stood for a moment looking down at the still surface of the water, silent and enchanted.

She looked very young and intensely, glowingly alive. Her violet eyes were clear and bright and she looked palpitatingly happy.

'You look really happy, my sweet, for the first time for weeks. This is how I always want to see you, not as a child of the shadows, but as a creature of sunlight with the beams trapped in your lovely golden hair,' said Curt, his eyes roving her face and appraising the halo of hair.

She laughed, answered him inconsequently.

'How sweet of you to think of taking a villa. But I would have been happy to stay with your mother.' She sighed with pure happiness. 'You're right, though, about living in the country, and I'm glad you're not a town owl like your mother. There's such a different atmosphere out in the country, an atmosphere which seems to me to cleanse the system of all town ills. Don't you agree?'

She sparkled up at him as he sat down sideways on the balustrade, and went willingly into the circle of the arms he held out to her.

'Darling,' he said slowly, the look in his eyes making her heart beat alarmingly fast, 'anywhere is heaven where you are. I know what you mean, though. There's an extraordinary atmosphere of timelessness, as if all those years since Adam and Eve had never happened. This luxurious villa and the fact that Henri will cook us a delicious dinner are material things compared with the spiritual needs.'

'Is that why you brought me here?' she asked him softly, framing his face with tender hands. 'Because I needed the peace of fresh surroundings to heal my broken heart?'

He reached for her wrists and, turning her hands, kissed each in turn before he spoke.

'I'm very proud of you, my sweet. You've suffered two terrible blows and have come up smiling. You've never gone around with a long face and bemoaned your loss.' He tweaked her small ear—his touch was very gentle—before he went on. 'Furthermore, you've never created a scene when I haven't been able to return home. I'm grateful, too, that tragedy hasn't made you bitter in any way. You're still soft and cuddly and beautifully wistful. Never change, my darling.'

'I won't,' she promised, winding her arms around his neck.

'Don't you want to see the other rooms?' he murmured against her mouth.

'We have all the time in the world to see them,' Felicity answered.

The villa was half an hour's run from Paris. Curt had rented it from a French sculptor of some repute, and his work was in alcoves throughout the villa and the gardens in perfect settings, where each work would show up to the best advantage. To Felicity, who was sensitive to beauty, the place was a never-ending source of delight.

Knowing how seldom Madame Moreau saw her son, she had insisted upon Curt going to fetch her to dine with them that evening. They had called on his mother on their arrival, also at Felicity's request, since she wished to thank his mother for her gifts and letters during the awful time she had spent in hospital and later after her other great loss.

Felicity knew Curt was pleased about it, and her reward was great to see him visibly relax in the company of her two most important women in his life. When she arrived, Madame Moreau looked beautifully chic and alluring in a little model dress in green velvet with emeralds at her throat and in her ears. She was enthusiastic about the villa; she knew the sculptor who owned it well.

'He's a genius, of course,' she said. 'He charges the earth to do a bust, but he'd probably want to do one of you free, Felicity. You have that kind of face.' She paused, and broke into a little laugh. 'Incidentally, he's crazy about beautiful women—but then he's got lots of charm that keeps them equally interested in him.'

'Sounds a real dish. Pity I shan't see the man,' Felicity said lightly.

'No, you won't. Curt didn't tell him he was bringing his wife. Did you, dear?' Madame Moreau teased.

'No. Being a Frenchman, he would probably want to sculpt her in the nude, and nobody is going to do that with my wife,' Curt answered with a deceptively lazy drawl.

They had coffee on the stone terrace after dinner, sitting in deep, low comfortable chairs piled with cushions, while Henri handed round the fragrant drink. It was a warm night, scented and mysterious, and away on the lake someone was playing a very French tune on an accordion. Felicity glanced at Curt seated on her left with his mother between them, and was vividly conscious of his presence and responsive to it. The tune floating across to them had changed to a romantic, dreamy but evocative note, and she watched him as he blew out grey scented wreaths of cigar smoke as she reclined in her chair.

There was something sphinx-like about his utter stillness as he sat there scarcely moving. She watched the clean-cut line of his jaw, seeing, with a thrill of pleasure, the hint of brutality, the arrogance to which she surrendered ecstatically. The light was changing almost imperceptibly until the lake was glossed with a luminous glow, and the villa and garden gradually took on an unearthly beauty.

'Who's for an hour on the lake?' asked Curt, and they rose eagerly.

At the boathouse, Curt strongly pulled out the boat on to the water and helped them in, tucking the cushions he had brought from the villa behind them. Then he boarded the craft agilely, steadying it as he sat down to reach for the oars. Peals of laughter came across to them from the far side of the lake where people were bathing; many like themselves had taken boats and were drifting idly on the calm water. There was a couple in a canoe, and Felicity thought they looked like honeymooners as they looked intently at each other, oblivious of the world about them.

The water had a dreamlike quality about it in the strange light shining on Curt's face and outlining the wide shoulders. Felicity leaned back, watching him pull steadily at the oars, aware that his mother was doing the same. She was obviously proud of her son and Felicity longed to ask about the other who had died, but she dropped the thought, seeing it as disloyal to Curt.

Presently they were drifting to the bank on the opposite side of the lake oars pulled in, the water lapping the sides of the boat. The laughing, splashing group of swimmers was very near, their voices ringing in the air with a joyful note. Then they were out of the boat on the bank and Curt was dragging it up on to the sandy earth. Together, they strolled to the gay little café painted white, with a flat roof where tubs of flowers could be seen decorating the edge.

The local wine was very palatable and they sat enjoying it and looking over the lake. Presently Felicity's eyes focused on a slender figure standing with her back to them looking across the water; something familiar in the poise of the uncovered red head reminded her of Nora Staffordly.

Felicity held her breath. Curt and his mother were talking together of some mutual friends who had taken a villa in Cannes. The woman's hair stirred gently in the breeze, and the profile she turned to Felicity as a man strolled up to join her left no doubt as to her identity. The couple turned and slowly made their way towards the café and she watched them approach wonderingly.

The man, heavily-built, had an insipid blondness. He seemed to have an air of boredom about him, Felicity caught herself thinking, and disliked him on sight. She could not have said who was first aware of the other, but the next moment the couple was there at their table, greeting Curt and Madame Moreau like old friends.

'Do join us,' Curt was saying. 'I believe you haven't yet met my wife, Clifford; Felicity, Clifford and Nora Staffordly.'

He was on his feet, drawing up two extra chairs to their table and signalling a waiter.

Felicity found herself looking into two rather small eyes set too close together, which looked her over appraisingly. For a moment she felt herself held by his gaze and the warm colour rushed up into her face. His pale grey eyes rested on her golden hair and traced the lines of her piquant face in a manner which she resented, but she greeted him charmingly, hoping that the casual meeting would not be repeated in the future.

'*Enchanté*, Madame Moreau,' he said, holding her slender hand closely in his grip. 'We have a villa here, our summer retreat, and I should be very happy if you would come and join us at one of our weekend parties. I'm sure Curt would enjoy the fishing. And you, madame, would find our swimming pool delightfully relaxing.'

'Our villa is on this side of the lake,' explained Nora. She was looking at Felicity kindly as she added, 'You would either have to come across the lake or drive round it in the car. However, I'm sure Curt will take it in his stride. I must say marriage suits him.' She turned to Curt, who was taking a bottle of wine and glasses from a hovering waiter. 'I've never seen him looking so well and relaxed.'

Felicity, seeing that look, wondered just how well Nora Staffordly did know Curt. Anyone of the dimmest intelligence could see the woman was shrewd, clever and calculating; whatever relationship Mrs Staffordly had with any man would be one that she could turn easily to her own account. Felicity knew she was no match for the woman and never would be. Consequently, her reply was rather stilted.

'As Curt has come here to work, I'm afraid we shan't be free to partake in much social life. His work is very demanding and it's for him to decide what we do with our leisure,' she said quietly.

Nora's laugh grated. 'Curt is never tired. I've never known a man of such abundant energy. Believe me, Curt can play as hard as he works. You don't know him yet.'

'*Touché*, Nora,' Curt grinned, passing her a glass of wine. 'You mustn't tell tales out of school.'

Fleeting Felicity recalled Blain's face on the day he had met her to say that Clifford Staffordly was divorcing his wife. Nora might be a friend of Curt's, but any friendship she herself had with the woman would only renew the heartache. She could not help but blame the woman for Blain's involvement into the whole affair. Fiercely she envied Nora Staffordly's friendship with Curt because it dated back long before she herself had known him. Did she really know her husband? Felicity was beginning to doubt it. It was Clifford Staffordly who spoke next, with his gaze on her flushed face.

'Marriage seems to suit your wife too, Curt,' he drawled. 'She's so fresh and sweet that I feel about ninety just looking at her.'

Madame Moreau smiled and chipped in, 'Yes, I have a lovely daughter-in-law. I hope Curt realizes how lucky he is.'

'Why should he?' Nora Staffordly leaned forward to the lighter Curt had flicked on for her cigarette. 'He has the natural instinct to choose the pick of everything. His valet Henri is perfection, like his clothes and his manners. Everyone always flocked to the parties he gave in his bachelor days, and he's made few mistakes. On the rare occasions that he has he hasn't hesitated to forget that mistake and cut his losses.' She blew out a line of smoke and watched it rise, her eyes hard. 'In fact, he can be quite ruthless once a venture has proved a failure, in immediately tossing it aside.'

'You appear to have me pretty well taped, Nora,' Curt said lightly. 'A man never amounts to much unless he does everything deliberately.'

Felicity had watched his face and he seemed in no way put out by the rather caustic statement. Was Nora's friendship with her husband the deep, long-lasting kind which allowed for such comments to be given and taken lightly? Or was there something at the bottom of it that was more deep-grained than Curt would have his listeners believe? He was not a man to wear his feelings in an expression for all to see. Felicity quelled a shiver. Had Mrs Staffordly been one of his mistakes which he had cast aside? There was no answer to that, nor likely to be.

Clifford Staffordly changed the conversation as he accepted another glass of wine, to satisfy what appeared to Felicity to be an insatiable thirst. He had listened silently to his wife's outburst with a cynical twist to his sensual mouth. He had admitted to feeling ninety earlier on, but it was a question if he would reach sixty at the rate he was going, the lines of dissipation around his thick jowl said that clearly, and he looked anything but a happy man. In fact, Felicity decided, they were a distinctly odd couple.

Neither of them stayed long, and they left repeating the invitation to pay them a visit at their villa. Upon returning across the lake Curt got out the car to take his mother back to Paris. Felicity did not offer to accompany them, thinking generously that his mother might care to have her son to herself once in a while, if only for a short time. But when they had gone she wandered about the bedroom consumed with a strange restlessness; suddenly she felt a strong nostalgia for the past as she had known it, with Blain and her parents at Norton Towers. There had been no problems there other than what to get for parties or birthday presents.

Tears rose weakly in her eyes as she clasped her elbows, mandarin fashion, in her pacing. She wanted Curt, of course, but she wanted her brother and mother too. Anna was always telling her that she could not have her cake and eat it, and she was doing just that. Poor Anna. No doubt she was missing the old life too, with Norton Towers so deserted.

How beautiful the garden was from the balcony of the room! When she had been young with Blain a garden was something of a challenge because there was such a lot to be discovered by the young in heart. Actually she was on a voyage of discovery and a kind of second honeymoon. What she had to discover was her real self; that self that existed without the family. She had to discover an entirely new person, who not only existed for Curt but for herself as well. It wasn't going to be easy, but her life now beckoned along strange paths which she must follow. There was no turning back since marriage to Curt had committed her to them.

And with this knowledge came the possibility that there would be things about Curt that she would discover too. But however unpalatable they might be she loved him, and with every nerve in her body wanted his lovemaking. Simply thinking about him brought a second rush of tears hurting her throat. Sleepily now, for the local wine was having its effect, Felicity prepared for bed. In spite of a troubled mind she was asleep as soon as her head touched the pillow, and never felt Curt slip into bed beside her much later.

They were having breakfast the next morning when Curt said casually,

'How did you feel meeting Nora Staffordly last night?'

Felicity gave her attention to her fruit juice. 'Not exactly delighted. Which isn't surprising, seeing what she did to Blain.'

Curt drank the last of his coffee and used the table napkin.

'I understand a little of what your feelings are, my sweet,' he answered evenly. 'However, the fact remains that, as Nora and I are old friends, it's essential for you to be friends with her also.'

Felicity put down her empty glass carefully. 'How long have you known her?'

'Since she was so high.' He gestured with a lean brown hand vaguely. 'We grew up together. Nora is three years older than I. You'll like her when you know her.'

'Will I?'

She looked at him with clear dark blue eyes and he shrugged, rising to his feet. Putting his chair against the table, he stood looking down at her with his hands curled around the back. Her golden hair was tied back with a blue ribbon, her wrap was blue with white nylon ruffles at her young throat and slender wrists. She looked very young and sweet, and very stubborn.

Very quietly he said, 'The past is past. Let it lie.'

Felicity trembled inwardly. 'There are things one can never forget. Nora Staffordly might be a friend of yours, but she can never be a friend of mine.'

His look hardened. 'You don't know the lady at all. Why not meet her with an open mind? She would be a good friend to you.'

Felicity left her chair and went to the balustrade of the terrace to grip it with trembling hands, presenting him with her slim back. Her voice was as low and controlled as she could make it.

'I understood that you brought me here to help me to forget the past, yet you're asking me to do the very thing which will bring it all back again. How dare you ask me to be friends with a woman of her character? Not only did she

126

do harm to my father by causing him endless worry, she almost wrecked Blain's life.'

'Blain was already wrecking his own life, or have you forgotten?'

Felicity swung round then, eyes blazing in a face pale as a magnolia. Her small nostrils dilated with anger. Curt had moved behind her and she looked up at him tense and quivering.

'I've forgotten nothing,' she blazed. 'I know you never liked Blain, but he was my brother and I loved him. Maybe you had good reason not to like him.'

'I had,' he answered laconically.

There was an electric silence, during which she stared up at his stern dark face.

'Because you were jealous.' The words tumbled from her lips without her being aware of speaking them.

Curt paled beneath his tan. 'Define "jealous",' he ordered.

Felicity stood her ground having gone beyond caution. 'You were jealous because he was Nora Staffordly's lover.'

Her wrist was suddenly seized in fingers of steel. 'Repeat what you've just said,' he demanded, and his tones were dangerously low. The blood had crept up beneath his tan and suddenly she was afraid, because he looked ready to do violence. Numb with terror, she watched him beat back the fury until there was nothing left but contempt in his eyes. His voice chilled her.

'Don't you ever judge me by that brother of yours again. I won't bother to deny what you've accused me of, but I shall demand an apology when I come back this evening to find you in a more normal frame of mind.' He flung her wrist out of his grasp and the imprint of his fingers was still there long after he strode away.

Standing there cold as a marble statue, Felicity heard him talking briefly to Henri, and soon after the roar of his car gradually hummed away into silence. Presently she groped for a chair at the table, and dropped into it, white and trembling. It was a long time before her eyes rested on her untouched breakfast. Her throat was dry and throbbing and her wrist, when she looked at it, bore the imprint of Curt's fingers in angry red marks.

'Fresh coffee, madame?'

Henri was there, his face enigmatic, with the fragrant brew, pouring out a cup for her. Then as discreetly as he had appeared, he left and went indoors. Felicity was too choked to eat, but she drank the coffee thirstily. After the second cup she felt better and made her way slowly to the bedroom.

Worn out emotionally as she was, it was not surprising that she slept at last, lying on the top of the bedclothes. Voices coming through her open window aroused her mid-morning—Clifford Staffordly enquiring if she was at home, and Henri replying that Madame's day was filled with engagements, but he would tell her of his visit. Felicity lay staring up at the ceiling as an intolerable weight of depression settled upon her, crushing her spirit. Her thoughts winged to her father and the ache to be with him was almost unbearable. Life suddenly seemed terribly hard and without purpose. Tears of self-pity rose to her eyes, and she brushed them away with an impatient hand. The four walls became a prison shutting her in and it was imperative to get out into the clear air. Yes, Henri told her, when later, she faced him cool and composed in a neat little safari-styled suit, there was a bus to Paris within the half hour.

The bus was filled with laughing, chattering people, making her feel her loneliness more acutely, but the winding road lay peaceful under the sun, the meadows sweet and colourful with flowers. Paris was as usual, a Circe whose beauty was a cure for all ills. The elegant Rue de Rivoli beckoned, but Felicity decided first to have lunch. By Métro she made her way to a charming place where Curt had taken her, where the walls were hung with sporting prints, in the Rue Duvivier which, she remembered, was close to the Ecole Militaire. Lunch was barbecued steak, cooked deliciously while you waited and served with potatoes done in their jackets.

Felicity had never felt less like eating, but at least it occupied her mind giving her no time for thought. Nevertheless, it was Curt's lean, dark face she saw in front of her as she ate mechanically. The red wine supplied with the lunch warmed her heart and she began to feel less melancholy.

Feeling much better with a satisfying meal inside her, Felicity strolled from the restaurant and passing the Ecole Militaire, continued down the green enchantment of the Champ de Mars beneath the arch of the Eiffel Tower and across the Pont d'Iéna. Then from the terrace of the Palais de Chaillot she gazed back enthralled on a very lovely view of the city. The shopping precincts occupied her thoughts for the rest of the afternoon and at last Felicity found herself on the bus returning once more to the villa.

She had left herself plenty of time to wash and change for dinner before Curt arrived home and, having done so, took a book and went out into the garden. It was impossible to read or even focus on anything apart from the fact that he would soon be home and he had to be faced. Their first quarrel and a very shattering one, since she had said unforgivable things. Her nerves were all wires stretched to snapping point when the sound of his car broke the stillness, and slowly the time passed during which her heart beat time to the ritual he went through, of washing and changing for the evening meal.

They met in the lounge. Wide-shouldered and elegant in evening dress, his skin deep brown, glowingly rich in health, Curt looked heartbreakingly dear. His cool glance at her slim figure in the simple white dress showing the apricot tan of her slender arms and youthful bare neck was enigmatic. There was no anger in his voice when he greeted her.

'Had a nice day?' he asked on the lift of an attractive

129

brow.

Felicity swallowed on a dry throat, and felt the little hard core of stubbornness melt away inside her. 'Oh, Curt darling,' she whispered, and the next moment his arms were around her as she crumpled against him.

'I'm sorry for what I said,' she mumbled as they stood there close, his cheek against her hair. 'Please say you're not angry any more.'

'I will be if you don't stop crying,' he murmured, kissing the tip of her small ear and moving his mouth down to her trembling lips.

His embrace was enchanting, his face firm and cool, his mouth warm and demanding. The old magic was there and he caught her up into his arms knowing that she was the most seductive woman he had ever known. He had known many beautiful women and he was too experienced—too down-to-earth—to admit that she was the most beautiful. But she was the most exciting, most beautiful being that had ever happened to him. She satisfied him in every way and was an unending delight with her elusive, feminine charm.

Taking her with him to the nearest chair he sat down, pulling her on to his lap, and his mouth moved caressingly again over her neck and face.

'You're as fresh as spring water,' he said, kissing a truant curl in her neck. 'There's a delicacy and fragrance about you, a natural sweetness. You're a witch, my sweet, luring me on until I'm not myself any more.'

She wound her arms around his neck, her heart a crazy machine out of control. 'That makes two of us,' she breathed against his mouth, moving her hands over his powerful shoulders. 'I love you.'

'You can say that again,' he said, then his mouth was burning hers with all the passionate longings and needs of a strong, virile man.

CHAPTER NINE

TIME passed pleasantly at the villa. Curt's behaviour left nothing to be desired; he was home on time in the evening and occupied himself in living up to every hour of the day. The good weather continued, days filled with sunshine when they lazed, walked or went sightseeing in the depths of the Chateau country. Madame Moréau came to see them often, and they visited her. So the daily routine of their life at the villa was an accepted thing. They had breakfast together before Curt left for his work in the city, and he was home on time in the evening, with an occasional day off during which he spent a few hours in his study dealing with his work back in London. There had been no mention of meeting the Staffordlys again and Felicity heard casually from Henri that they had gone away on holiday.

One of Felicity's greatest delights was the lake, where she swam often or sat smiling on the terrace as she watched the bathers and the gay boats sailing on the water. She wrote often to her father, who like herself had needed a respite from surroundings which had oppressed them. He had friends at his club and lots of things to distract him. Yes, she thought, watching heads bobbing up and down in the sparkling water, everyone at some time or another in their lives needed a break. Life was always changing and adjustments were necessary. How much easier it was if one could go away and dissect their former life, thus putting it into a true perspective in order to accept the change.

On one of his days off from work, Curt took her to Paris and bought her a car. It was a Renault. 'I'll arrange for you to sell your car back home when we return,' he said, 'there are too many memories of Blain and your mother for you to keep it and be happy.'

He had taken her out for the day in it, insisting upon her driving herself in order to become used to the brakes. 'Thank heaven you're a good driver. I shall have nothing to worry about when you're out during the day.' It was a day like many others in Curt's company all the more enjoyable because he knew his way about.

'One of the greatest charms about a day out,' he said, 'is driving along an uncluttered country road and spotting the kind of place where you know you're going to dine well and enjoy it. The small country hotels are the jewels in the crown of France, and their hospitality and food is second to none.'

They drove through dense oak, pine and beech woods, ideal for picnicking, and from a rise on the road gazed down on stately castles and gushing streams just asking for fishermen. The air was like wine when they left the car to stretch their legs and breathe in the scent of blossom by a flowing river.

Curt stood with an arm around Felicity's shoulders and bent his head to breathe in her fragrance.

'You're like a child of the sun,' he murmured into her hair, 'all gold and shining.'

Felicity reached up a small hand to caress his hard cheek. 'I always want to be in the sun with you, never in the shadow.'

They came upon the little hotel, snuggled in a nest of tall trees overlooking a delightful small village. Their host's greeting could not have been more cordial. Courteously, on a little bow, his eyes twinkling, he said, 'Monsieur and Madame are very welcome. I trust the country air has sharpened your appetites.'

Curt took her arm and followed him into a dining-room filled deliciously with the tantalizing aroma of good cooking.

'Simple home-made fare,' said their host, serving them with a creamed vegetable soup, a rough country pâté, an omelette of meat and mushrooms cooked in a wine sauce, casserole of chicken with mixed vegetables, strawberries and cream and a bottle of local wine.

Curt's wink, his casual, half-bullying manner in trying to make her eat, made Felicity feel on the edge of laughter. One course followed another, with their host smiling on them as he put it down as if he was glad of giving them the opportunity of enjoying themselves. The wine, white and ice-cold, was a delicious drink to Felicity, who felt as if the cool freshness of a mountain stream was trickling down her throat.

Curt raised his glass with a twinkle. 'Here's to us. We must do this often.'

Life's tragedy; the bitter disappointments and disillusionments, faded as in a dream. Too dazed by happiness, Felicity smiled at him dreamily, and finished her glass. He grinned and refilled their glasses. By the time she had finished her second glass, she knew it was one of those perfect days which could never be recaptured, except in delicious memories.

Later that afternoon they motored to a cool spot and lay in the shade, blissfully content. In the fields, the hay waved like a moving golden sea and Felicity came to him on long golden legs with armfuls of yellow daisies and crimson clover. The sun was setting when they returned, and as the gold faded to rose, giving way eventually to a dark turquoise, the villa welcomed them, a white shape against the deepening sky and twinkling stars.

Felicity learned from Curt that the case he was working on was going well, and would probably be over in about three to four months after all, instead of the six months he had expected. While she knew that the present idyllic existence could not go on for ever, she wanted it to last as long as possible with nothing to spoil it. Three months of their visit had already gone when one evening they went across the lake by boat after dinner, for a glass of the local wine from the lakeside restaurant.

They had strolled back to the boat and Curt had pushed it out on the water when a voice called to them; Clifford and Nora Staffordly were on the terrace of the restaurant they had just left, leaning on the balustrade looking down on them. Nora was hatless, and her hair was tucked behind her ears, emphasizing the lovely curve of her neck and face. Against the bright cotton dress, her bare arms and throat were tanned to a golden brown.

Her husband was also bareheaded and deeply tanned, giving his hair a more nondescript look than it usually had. His glance lingered on Felicity. He said something to his wife and smiled and looked at her again, his eyes narrowing in a way that made Felicity glad she was with Curt. There was something about Clifford Staffordly that made her shiver.

He shouted a greeting which Curt answered, resting on his oars before putting them into play. Nora waved; but it was not a happy carefree gesture, and Felicity was startled by her drawn look of unhappiness. Again she felt a twinge of something rather tragic about the lovely face. She could hardly be fretting for Blain, since he had been only one of her many affairs. Why then did she look so unhappy? Was her marriage really to blame, or was Curt the cause? A cool breeze caught them as Curt used an oar to push the boat away from the side after lifting a hand in a final wave to the Staffordlys. Felicity quelled a shiver as something seemed to wing itself over the brightness of her day. Her happiness had been so complete until now. It had occurred to her more than once that, as Nora Staffordly lived just across the lake, it was inevitable that they would meet—the holiday they had taken was evidently over. Yet she had perversely shied away from any thought of them coming back before Curt's work was finished.

She looked across at him under her lashes, at the wide shoulders, strong upper arms with muscles rippling beneath as he pulled lazily on the oars. He had shown no more than the usual amount of surprise and pleasure at meeting old friends, but then he was excellent at hiding his emotions. Was she misjudging him? Had she so far left her girlhood behind that she was fast becoming a jealous wife? Heaven forbid!

Some urge inside her moved her lips to form a question about the Staffordlys, but her deep love for him had not altogether banished her shyness. One intent look from his eyes and she was sunk. It was something that had to be conquered, because until it was she was just putty in his hands; he could do whatever he liked with her.

'Is Clifford Staffordly an . . . alcoholic?' she managed at last.

Curt frowned, and said tolerantly, 'Whatever made you ask that question?'

'Is he?'

His eyes moved slowly over her golden hair, gleaming softly against the background of dark trees.

'He was,' he admitted somewhat unwillingly.

'You don't like him,' said Felicity.

'He doesn't like me either.'

She lifted candid blue eyes to his enigmatic face. 'But you like Mrs Staffordly.'

'Yes,' laconically.

She lay back in her seat and trailed her fingers through the water, trying to subdue the tumult of feeling threatening to choke her. She wanted to think that any intimate association Curt had had with Mrs Staffordly was a passing thing, that was over now that he was married; but she could not believe this, not with this sickening fear swamping all other emotions. That brief contact with Nora, a cataclysmic re-entry of the woman into her life, had alerted her to seeing herself as a person trained to control emotions and to ignore violent feelings.

Her convictions dissolved into doubts. Was she wrong?

Was she mistaking a casual friendliness for something much deeper? Felicity had a horror of making a scene and disclosing her own personal feelings, even to Curt. Suppose the whole thing was a fantasy of her own imagination?

The beauty of the night was all around them. In such ideal surroundings how could she have base thoughts? Curt was hers now—the gold band on her finger assured her of this. Her eyes moved again to his face as he pulled easily on the oars, loving everything about him, his dark, exciting looks, his keen, intent gaze, his arrogance, the mockery in his eyes, his courtesy and unfailing charm. Soon she would lie in his arms, and the thought blotted out everything else. The past, like the future, did not count; for her there was just going to be the present—golden months, weeks, possibly days now of being alone together with the rest of the world forgotten. When he had put the boat away, Curt came to where she stood on the terrace.

'You're like a beautiful statue of the Madonna,' he whispered, breaking off a flower from a trailing vine around one of the stone pillar supports, and threading it gently in her hair. 'But please come to life.'

The scent of flowers lay heavily on the still air and the garden was drowned in moonlight, clear and white. The night closed them in with its mystery, its warmth and its romance.

Curt bent slowly over her, drawing her unresisting into his arms. His eyes narrowed and a gleam came into them, making the blood run swiftly through her veins. He spoke softly.

'The night is ours, my sweet. It's beckoning us in. Can you hear it?'

'Yes, I hear it.' Slowly her arms stole around his neck and he bent his head still further, shutting out all things disturbing. Then, with his lips on hers, he swept her up into his arms and carried her swiftly indoors.

*   *   *

Felicity loved the heat, absorbing it in like a ripening peach. In the fields sloping down from the villa gardens to the lake harvesters were at work cutting down the long golden corn. Dreamily from her seat on the terrace, she watched young men with brown torsoes wielding scythes and cutting the long stalks close to the soil. Lost in the rhythm of the swung curved blade, Felicity was admiring the skill and energy of a craft so seldom seen in the modern age when a voice behind her startled her into turning round.

'Mrs Moreau,' Clifford Staffordly said smoothly, 'I came to ask if you wanted a lift into the city. I'm on my way there, and would be delighted to give you a lift.'

Native caution kept Felicity from showing her dislike, but her voice as she replied said it for her.

'Thanks, Mr Staffordly, but I have my own car. It's very kind and thoughtful of you to think of me, but no,' she said firmly.

Unabashed, he smiled. 'Some other time, perhaps?' he suggested, his colourless brows lifted hopefully in a query.

'I'm afraid not,' was the cool answer.

In his lightweight beige trousers, sandals and an open-necked silk shirt with the monogram of his old school on the breast pocket—well-cut clothes which he wore carelessly—he could not have looked a more pleasant neighbour. He was standing against one of the stone pillars covered with flowering vines which supported the roof, his thumbs tucked into the top of his trousers. If he was angry, he was covering his anger with an assumed nonchalance.

'I'm sorry you've been warned off me,' he said with an ugly slant to his rather loose mouth, 'too bad. You and I might have had some good times together.'

Felicity stiffened. 'I've not been warned off you. It so happens that I'm a married woman and I don't require men friends, especially married ones.'

'A one-sided loyalty if ever I saw one. Too bad your husband doesn't reciprocate.'

137

Felicity's heart moved in her chest until she could hardly breathe.

'What do you mean?'

'My wife—your husband—surely you know? They've always been in love with each other. I feel sorry for Nora, since she hasn't a hope this side of eternity in getting hold of him.'

'I don't believe a word of it. You're lying!'

The words tumbled from Felicity's lips before she could prevent them.

'Then what's your version? You think that he cares for her. I'm sure she cares for him. You think perhaps he has only amused himself with her in the past?'

In a turmoil of feeling, she tried to control herself. 'You'd better go, and take your evil insinuations with you. How right I was in refusing to further our acquaintance! Get out!'

Unable to suffer his company a moment longer, Felicity escaped along the terrace and round the corner of the villa. She glanced at the men below, still at work in the fields, then turned down one of the pretty walks leading to the boathouse by the lake. She was profoundly shocked by the confirmation of her worst fears. There was a gate at the bottom of the garden opening on to a path, but she leaned on the gate like one who had been running, believing everything Clifford Staffordly had told her.

No wonder Curt had accepted the chance to work in Paris, since Nora Staffordly was there! She recalled that afternoon with her mother in the London salon, when she had told Nora that she was expecting a baby. There had been the same bleak look on Nora's face as when she had looked down at them the previous evening at the restaurant.

Entirely possessed by the tragic, lovely face of Nora Staffordly, Felicity stood motionless for a very long time, then slowly made her way back to the villa. By the time she had showered and chosen her dress for the evening, the shock of what Clifford Staffordly had said was less acute.

Her dress, a floating grey chiffon, deepened the blue of her eyes, and as she put on the beaten gold necklace and matching bracelet, thoughts of the last time she wore them came flooding back. Her birthday ball. For fleeting moments Blain was somewhere near; she saw him again, meeting her in the hall, his eyes roving over her with the old audacious appraisal. He was strolling with Elvira in the garden, riding to meet her for an early morning canter. She knew again the old, happy expectation, wiped completely away by the painful pang of loss and pain burning inside her.

The chiming of the old French clock in the hall downstairs broke in on her thoughts. She looked at her watch and saw that it was seven o'clock; Curt was late, very late. Maybe he had been delayed and was already on his way— silly to be anxious because he had not telephoned. With her dress billowing around her in a cloudy mist, Felicity went downstairs, aching to see the tall, immaculate, swift-moving figure that for her was the whole meaning of her existence.

And there it was, the sound of the car. Her heart leapt, faltered, then hammered on into her ribs as she ran to the door. At first she only saw a blur of white floating demurely beside Curt's smart city-going suit.

'I'm sorry,' Nora Staffordly was saying, 'but I insisted on coming with Curt to make my apologies for keeping him so late at his chambers. I do hope you forgive me. I'm so sorry, we didn't notice the time.'

Curt had stood aside to enable Nora to precede him into the hall and she did so, offering her hand to Felicity with a piquant graciousness.

Felicity accepted it with a half-believing smile. She had stiffened perceptively. Then Curt was looking down at her, lean, mocking and narrow-eyed.

'Hello, my sweet, sorry I'm late. I suggest we punish

139

Nora by making her stay and share the delayed dinner,' he drawled in persuasive tones.

His kiss was cool and confident, and it was on the tip of her tongue to suggest Mrs Staffordly had probably made other arrangements. But a fleeting glance at the very pretty all-occasions dress, cream linen with a halter neck, so flattering to the lovely shoulders tanned to perfection, told her that Nora had come prepared to stay. Curt's smile was cool and infuriating and Felicity teetered; it was no use thinking of any sympathy or assistance from him.

Very calmly she said, 'Will you take Mrs Staffordly upstairs to the guest room? I must go to tell Henri that we have a guest for dinner.'

She had not looked up at Curt, in case his eyes were still on the radiant creature so near to his shoulder. Instead, her smile, quite an effort, had been trained on her unexpected guest.

Dinner that evening was a desperately unhappy meal for Felicity, although Curt was his usual charming, attentive and amusing self, showing only too clearly his fascination for Nora Staffordly. During the meal she observed her guest with painful curiosity, endeavouring to see her with fresh eyes as though seeing her beauty for the first time, and thus feeling, as Curt must have done, the fresh impact of her charm.

Curt and Blain: both had been victims of that charm of red hair and dulcet tones. She was aware of Nora speaking.

'I'm terribly sorry, Mrs Moreau, about your tragic loss. Not only of your baby, but also of your mother and brother—how shattering it must have been for you,' she was saying sympathetically.

Felicity, in a turmoil of feeling, was momentarily bereft of words. It was Curt who answered.

'Thanks, Nora,' he said quietly, firmly. 'We're finding our visit here all the more resting, since it gives us the

140

opportunity to relax and put past sorrows behind us. More wine? Felicity and I are growing increasingly fond of the local brew, but we daren't ask Henri to serve it. He would be shocked.' His teeth flashed into a white grin as she re-filled her glass, but Felicity refused a second.

Nora took the hint and followed his lead away from a painful subject. So the evening wore on, with Felicity smiling, talking and graciously listening, upheld by one strong surge of determination to show nothing to Nora of her own fear and unhappiness. Her look at Curt when he had rescued the conversation from Nora's condolences, had been so grateful that he had raised startled brows, taken aback by its beauty. He had been gentle and teasing in turn, bestowing upon her rather curious looks which she had very carefully avoided. It was a relief, therefore, when he left the villa with his guest to drive her home by car around the lake. They had driven away like a ship into the night, leaving Felicity feeling stranded on an island of desolation, alone.

Numbly, she wandered out on to the terrace to gaze un-seeingly across the still waters of the lake as dark now as her thoughts. Voices drifted from the direction of the res-taurant on the far side, punctuated by laughter and song. Where did one go from here? she asked herself in despair. Admit defeat and go away, or stay and share her husband with another woman? The latter course was unthinkable.

Felicity pushed her hair back from an aching head. Her emotions were too ragged, too confused to think clearly. All she could think of was that Curt's strength, his tenderness and companionship were her life. She needed him so much in her lost little world, with no niche save the one he had carved out for her. She could not live without his love. That being so, there was no alternative but to fight for that love. Felicity was no coward, but she was also proud, too proud to fight for a man who preferred another woman. She lifted her left hand and drove her right fist into it in her anguish.

She thought of him being with Nora in the intimacy of his car, Curt of the flashing smile and mocking eyes, so unbearably attractive when one loved him, and Nora did. Why, after the affair with Blain, had she had anything to do with the woman at all? And why had she not told Curt to forbid her to the house? Because her love for him made her weak where he was concerned. But she would be weak no longer; she would have it out with him tonight when he returned. With this thought in mind, Felicity drifted unhappily to the lounge. There she drew open the curtains and looked out into the night, drawing in deep breaths of air as she opened the French windows.

She heard the car, and presently he came striding into the room with his usual air of disciplined grace as she turned from the window.

He smiled and put out his hand. 'Come here, my sweet. Tell me what you've been doing all day, and why you looked so cross when I arrived with Nora.'

'Cross!' Felicity swallowed indignantly. 'I like that! You bring that woman here, admitting that she was the reason for you coming in late, and ask me why I looked so cross. Why was any of it necessary? Please tell me that.'

He saw that she was white and trembling, and knew that the obvious thing to do was to take her in his arms and silence her with kisses. But he was not going to allow any woman to order him to do anything, least of all his wife.

In clipped tones he stated, 'Mrs Staffordly is a friend of mine, and I don't have to explain anything to you. What's got into you? I've never seen you like this before. You've always been so sweet.'

'And so tractable. Why didn't you finish? That's been the trouble. You do just what you please.'

Suddenly he was taut, and speaking with a deadly quietness. 'Now look here, Felicity. I refuse to quarrel with you over such a small thing as bringing a friend home and asking her to stay to dinner.'

'When that friend happens to be an old flame who's still burning brightly, I can hardly see you regarding bringing her home as a small thing.' Felicity clenched trembling hands. 'What would you have said had I arrived home late with Clifford Staffordly, and made the same excuse as you that we hadn't noticed the time?'

'That's entirely a different thing,' he said tersely.

'You bet your life it is!' she flung at him. 'I happen to have more respect for my married state than you. I'll have you know that I could have done just the same with Clifford Staffordly, but I happen to have more respect than to mix with his kind.'

'I'm sure you have, my sweet, which goes to show how much you love me,' he said cajolingly, holding out his hand again. 'Come and kiss me, and put an end to a silly little upset. I refuse to let the Staffordlys come between us any way.'

'You brought her here, I didn't,' she insisted.

'Come here,' he commanded.

But Felicity didn't move. 'Why were you so late coming home? What was so important that you didn't notice the time? I have a right to know,' she told him obstinately.

'As an old friend, Nora was seeking my advice. I did notice the time, but I couldn't turn her away when she needed my help.'

Felicity lifted her chin defiantly. 'I'm sure you could-n't ...'

Her next words were stifled into silence as Curt hauled her into his arms and crushed her mouth with his own. She gasped and stiffened in his arms, and he released her slowly.

'Doesn't that convince you that I love you and not Nora?' he demanded. 'What's the matter with you?' His eyes narrowed thoughtfully. 'Just a minute—you men-tioned Clifford Staffordly. What's he been telling you?'

Felicity tried to push him away, but his arms were an iron band around her and he refused to release her altogether.

Grimly she said, 'We're talking about tonight, remember? You haven't told me what was so important that you came home late, then asked Mrs Staffordly to stay to dinner.'

He let her go then, pushing his hands into his pockets and looking down on her with a deep frown. 'Is that why you're holding away from me? You've never done that before. Are you using this evening as an excuse for us not to be close?'

Felicity was aghast. 'How can you say that, when you know I love you more than anything else in the world?'

His expression softened and he gripped her shoulders, looking into her eyes searchingly.

'Then what is it?' he demanded.

'Oh, Curt! Don't you see it's Mrs Staffordly? She has such a reputation for affairs, and you won't tell me why she made you late coming home this evening.'

He shook her gently. 'I'm a barrister, my sweet. What happened between Mrs Staffordly and myself is confidential and personal. I'm bound by my profession not to disclose anything concerning my work in that respect.' His mouth tightened. 'Besides, giving in to your demand now could set a precedent for the future which I have no intention of giving in to. I'm master in my own house. Do you understand?'

Felicity went white to the lips. 'I understand all right, but I refuse to share you with another woman. Do you understand that?'

She tried to wriggle out of his grasp, and found it impossible as he gave a short laugh.

'What's this? You little idiot! Do you think I enjoyed having Mrs Staffordly here tonight? We see little enough of each other, you and I, as it is. I had something to tell you

144

too.'

She looked at him hopefully. 'What is it?'

He drew her into his arms and his mouth found hers casually, experimentally, and lingered briefly. 'Do you still love me?'

She went willingly into the haven of his arms, which would always hold magic for her, and pressing her slenderness against him, kissed him passionately.

'Now tell me your news,' she said when at last she was able to draw breath. 'You know you've never been in any doubt about my feelings for you.'

'My work here is nearly at an end, and this week should see it through. Some time next week we shall be flying home to Cherry Trees. We shall be settled in by the time the Colonel returns. You'll want to be there to welcome the poor old chap, won't you?'

'Of course. Oh, Curt, it's going to be heaven to be back home again with you!'

She shone up at him, and he smiled down at her mockingly. 'You haven't asked me if Nora is coming with us?' he teased.

Felicity's eyes glittered, and she struck at his chest with clenched hands. 'You beast,' she cried, 'I could kill you!'

He laughed. 'Why not kiss me instead?' he murmured, drawing her closer.

CHAPTER TEN

ANNA was waiting to meet them at Cherry Trees, for Curt had telephoned to ask her to fill the house with flowers for when they returned. With her kind face beaming and her hair just a little greyer, Anna greeted Felicity with a hug and a tear or two.

'There's a present for you in your room,' she whispered conspiratorially, 'I'd love to see what it is before I go.'

And while Curt and Henri busied themselves with the paraphernalia from the cars, they ran upstairs together.

Anna was a little out of breath and sat down on the bed while Felicity untied the cord from a large square box to reveal the silky richness of a fur coat, a fabulous mink. It was from Curt.

'Oh, isn't it gorgeous!' Felicity cried ecstatically, as Anna helped her into it. 'How like Curt not to say a word about it!'

She was rubbing her face caressingly against the snug collar when Henri appeared with her cases and, shedding the coat, Felicity lost no time in opening one to give Anna her presents.

'I'll give Daddy his when I come over to Norton Towers,' she told Anna, as she loaded her with presents from Curt and herself.

The Colonel came home to Norton Towers in the autumn to a carpet of fallen leaves in beautiful colours of brown, orange, flame and yellow, at his feet. Felicity was there to greet him with Anna, and Curt came later to dinner.

Winter at Norton Towers had meant rides over the hard earth, crunchy walks through the crisp snow and shared nights before a big blazing log fire. Felicity, remembering these things, watched her father anxiously over dinner on his first evening home. He seemed little changed, he even laughed occasionally, but the laughter never reached his eyes. Like me, she thought, he will never quite lose the aching longing in his heart to see his loved ones and to hear their voices again.

She trembled to think of her own happiness, with the feeling that she had no right to it. It was so complete, so perfect, that she was afraid to accept it. It could not be real.

'It's real enough,' Curt assured her, when she confided her doubts to him in the soft darkness of their bed. 'Just take it with both hands and be happy.'

So gradually Felicity's customary good sense prevailed and she realized that in order to enjoy her own happiness it was essential to see her father happy too. She went to Norton Towers every day to walk with him in the grounds, so poignantly lovely now in their autumn colours, and encouraged him to invite his friends in to play chess with him in the evenings. The little Sealyham pup, Whisky, became his constant companion and nothing had been so important to Felicity than to see her father's eyes light up when she came to visit him.

'I'm getting to be an old man, my dear,' he told her on one occasion. 'You mustn't spend so much of your time with me. You have a husband and a home of your own, and soon there'll be children.'

He looked at her and smiled meditatively, and she felt the hot colour rush beneath her clear skin.

'Perhaps ... perhaps I shan't have any more,' she faltered. 'I had my chance and threw it away.'

'Nonsense.' He patted her shoulder comfortingly. 'You're healthy, and there's no reason why you shouldn't have children. Have you talked to Curt about it?'

Felicity shook her head. 'I haven't really got around to it. He's so busy with his work. He's a very popular man,

147

Daddy.'

He nodded his head. 'I know, and clever. Too clever.' He smiled rather sadly at her startled blue gaze and the query in her eyes. 'It's all right, my dear. He's a good man but brilliant. Forgive the brutal candour, but I've always felt that you would have been much happier married to someone with a less demanding career. I know you have a nature that's vulnerable, and you're bound to get hurt.'

She patted his hand as it lay on her shoulder and felt it tremble.

'I'm very happy, Daddy, so stop worrying about me. I love Curt and there'll never be any other man for me. None of us can go through life without being hurt, and I've been very lucky in my family and in my husband.'

Felicity knew this was true. Curt was never too busy, even though his work came home with him, to look after her with a tenderness that saw her smallest wants granted. He lived in a world of briefs and telephone calls, but it never occurred to her to hate his work for taking up so much of his life. He was a man of intense, driving physical energy, an energy needing an outlet in a demanding job. He was also a man with deep feelings and emotions and he had disciplined himself to hold the latter in check. Curt was a man who worked hard and played hard; there were no half measures with him.

Henri, soft-footed and, like his master, mercilessly efficient, ran the house on oiled wheels. He asked virtually nothing since Curt was kind, considerate and very generous to him and the rest of the staff. He gave them generous holidays and chose their presents personally at Christmas along with Felicity, who had expected him to be impatient with shopping, or, like her brother, humorously patient. But he had let her buy things freely, never demurring about the cost, and nothing he bought was second rate.

Easter came and with it the magic of waking trees and flowers, the insistent demands of hungry young birds, the

148

scent of clover, mists of bluebells and the gold of daffodils. The maternity ward in the tree outside the nursery window was full to overflowing. Felicity could hear the baby birds demanding food as she cut flowers for the house. Nearby Joe, the old gardener, looked up at the tree with a twinkle in his eyes.

'No birth pills up there, I reckon,' he chuckled, and went on tending his roses.

At the Easter recess, Curt brought his clerk home with him for the weekend. He had been with him since he took up office, an attractive young man in his twenties whose unusual colouring of dark brows and lashes and fair hair spoke of French blood. His name was Roger Vallet.

'*Enchanté*, Mrs Moreau,' he exclaimed when Curt smilingly introduced them. 'I wish all my working weekends were as pleasant as this one.'

'I hope Curt doesn't work you too hard,' she said demurely, liking his boyish shyness and his appraisal of herself.

'I'm lucky to work with Mr. Moreau,' he answered gravely. 'It's an honour.'

Apparently they were engaged on an important case and Curt was in a hurry to finish it. So the two men worked until lunch time each day and Felicity went to Norton Towers to see her father. On Saturday evening Felicity gave a small dinner party partly for the benefit of their guest; the Colonel and Judge Greatman were there, and it had been a great success.

On Sunday evening Roger went over to Norton Towers at the Colonel's invitation, and after dinner Felicity was sitting with Curt in the lounge enjoying their favourite records. Curt had poured out drinks and, after giving Felicity hers, sat down beside her on the couch.

'I shall have to stay at my chambers next week,' he began, looking down into his drink. 'I shall be in court during the day and in the evening there'll be too much to do

149

to come home.'

'Oh, Curt! Must you?'

Her look was piteously appealing. Curt swallowed part of his drink.

'I'm afraid I must, my sweet, there's nothing else for it. Don't be too upset.' He put an arm around her and drew her head on to his chest. 'It will only be a matter of about four days, then we can arrange a holiday. What do you say to that?'

She smiled up at him. 'That will be wonderful. Where shall we go?'

'What about the Greek island where we spent our honeymoon?'

'Oh, yes, please,' she gasped with delight.

'And while I'm away you can shop for it.' He kissed the top of her head. 'Am I forgiven?'

Felicity lifted her chin and nodded. When his mouth came down hard on her own she felt that nothing in the world existed but their completeness in each other, his lips on hers and his arms possessing her with their steely strength. When the kiss ended she snuggled against him, warm and loving, and listened to the music filling the room.

He was away a week, during which time Felicity missed him dreadfully. The Colonel had friends in now most evenings to play chess with him, and she spent her evenings at Cherry Trees alone. She ran through a gamut of emotions she had experienced at no time in her life before, and could hardly wait as the time drew near for his return home at the weekend.

She had not gone shopping for holiday clothes during his absence, as he had suggested, preferring to wait until he could accompany her. Shopping, like everything else, was so much more fun with Curt. There were moments during his absence which gave her food for thought on the way he was taking over her life. It was moments like these that made her realize how strong the bond was between them. It was sufficient for Henri to mention his name to send her heart leaping with the sense of delight his presence always gave her.

When Saturday dawned, Felicity awoke with the realization that Curt was coming home and she would see him within a few hours. So, after an exhilarating ride on Sandy, she sat down to breakfast and picked up the morning paper. And there it was in large type across the front page. *Wealthy Financier found dead.*

Clifford Staffordly had been found dead in the lounge of his villa just outside Paris on Friday morning by a maid. Foul play had not been ruled out.

Felicity started to tremble. The words were frightening because they were so conclusive, and she read the smaller print with a sense of shock. There was reason to believe he had been poisoned. Poor man! Although she had never liked him, Felicity was sorry, and she wondered if Curt had seen it. Torn by conflicting emotions, she put the paper down determined to put the matter out of her mind. It was nothing to her that Clifford Staffordly had died from suspected food poisoning; the only thing was she hoped he had not suffered, since it was a dreadful way to die.

Her thoughts immediately flew again to Curt, perhaps telephoning to Paris for more details since Nora Staffordly was his friend. Silly of her to imagine him dashing off to Paris: I have to forget this thing I have about him and Nora, she told herself. And she wasn't going to allow the news of the tragedy to upset her, she decided. But as the day wore on and Curt did not arrive, Felicity grew restless and unable to settle to anything for long.

By the time the telephone rang, early that evening, her nerves were stretched to breaking point.

'Hello! Is that you, Curt?' she asked with bated breath.

'Yes, my sweet. I'm in Paris.'

A sense of shock washed over her. 'Paris?' she echoed stupidly. 'What are you doing there? Surely you were coming home today?'

'I was,' laconically. 'I can't explain over the telephone. I'll be seeing you tomorrow.' He paused, then added, 'I take it you've seen the morning papers?'

'Yes, I have,' she answered dully, trying to take in the fact that not only had he gone to Paris without asking her to go with him, he had gone without telling her. He had not even given her the chance to go with him. She put down the phone and clasped her shaking hands together. Had Nora sent for him, or had he gone of his own accord? Whichever way it was he was there with her now. They would probably be spending the evening together, rediscovering each other, finding again the magic in each other that had never actually died but which had remained smouldering.

That evening, because she could not bear her own company any longer, Felicity went to Norton Towers to see her father. Directly the Colonel saw her so soon after dinner, he knew there was something worrying her.

'Isn't Curt with you?' he asked, seeing the new look on her face replacing the old one of radiant happiness.

'He's working,' she said, sitting down on a chair facing him by the fireplace, and accepting a drink.

She had been hoping he had not noticed, and she wanted to keep her troubles from him. But though some men are usually unobservant about such things, the Colonel was quick to notice the change.

'Is anything wrong, my dear?' he asked, sitting down in his chair, glass in hand.

Felicity bit her lip, and her face was expressionless as she fixed her eyes on Whisky curled up on the carpet at her father's feet. It was terribly hard to know what to say without the feeling that somehow she was betraying Curt by talking about him.

'I suppose you've seen the morning paper,' she began, choosing her words carefully, 'about Nora Staffordly's husband?'

He nodded. 'A bad business,' was his comment.

'Curt has gone to Paris, presumably to see Mrs Staffordly. I'm worried about him.'

'Why?'

Felicity shot him a surprised glance. He seemed quite unperturbed. Her answer came indignantly with a question. 'You approve?'

'I neither approve nor disapprove, since Curt is a Q.C. and an eminent one. I suppose Mrs Staffordly is suspect number one concerning her husband's death,' he said mildly.

Felicity looked startled. Her deep blue eyes widened to their fullest extent, and she nearly spilled her drink.

'You meant Curt could have gone with the intention of defending her? The thought never crossed my mind that she could have had anything to do with her husband's death.'

The Colonel looked at her thoughtfully. 'Why else did you think he had gone to Paris?'

Her face flooded with colour beneath his scrutiny. 'Nora Staffordly and Curt are old friends,' she said in a low voice. 'He's admitted to being fond of her to me, his wife. With a woman of her reputation, what is one to deduct from that?'

Her father smiled at her gently. 'That they're old friends. My dear, Curt is a dangerously attractive man where the fair sex are concerned; he must have had endless affairs in his youth. Nora Staffordly was one of them. All his other affairs have gone, and you aren't concerned with them because you know nothing about them. Mrs Staffordly is the one you happen to know personally, so she looms up as a very real threat to your peace of mind.'

'And my marriage,' Felicity finished for him. 'Why should he be the one to defend her? There are many excellent men who could do the job just as well.'

'He might have some reason for acting for her,' said the Colonel satirically.

Irritably Felicity said, 'Why don't you be more explicit, instead of leaving a question hanging in the air?'

'Because, my dear, I know no more about the matter than you do. I will say this, though, I'm willing to back you against Nora Staffordly any time. You're Curt's wife, don't forget that.'

'Marriages,' answered Felicity darkly, 'are of the egg-shell kind today, easily broken.'

To which her father answered, 'And nothing is so dead as a dead love, my dear.' He smiled wisely. 'And don't look for things that aren't there. I can name several very eligible young men who are still in love with you; David Colston, and two whom I won't name with titles, for example.'

'I don't believe you. Besides, I haven't been out with any of them since my marriage.' She smiled at him fondly. 'It's nice of you, Daddy, to cheer me up.'

And the Colonel wisely left it at that.

Felicity awaited Curt's arrival the following day with mixed feelings. To begin with she was angry with him for doing what he had done without any thought to herself. Nora Staffordly did not bother her so much. If she was to be charged with murder, then the woman would need all the help, she could get—but not from Curt. Felicity was determined about that. She thought of Curt despairingly, remembering how fatally easy it was to succumb to his virile, overpowering attraction. Achingly she wanted to feel the strength and comfort of his arms around her and seek forgetfulness in his lovemaking, but his actions had started a train of thought that could not be lulled into a feeling other than false security. I won't run to meet him, she told herself, and with this thought in mind she was out longer than usual that morning, riding on Sandy. The air was crisp and cool through her gold wool sweater, but when she dismounted at the stables there was heat in her cheeks as she ran a finger around the high polo neck.

After rubbing Sandy down, Felicity put her cheek

against his head, wishing she felt as placid and content as he did. The old tree sheltering them from the sun overhead rustled gently, and she let the peace of the musk-scented stables wash over her. She never heard the car.

Curt came towards her and the blood drummed through her body. Her heart lurched as he smiled down at her with his usual breathtaking charm.

Suddenly, the voice she heard speaking did not seem to belong to her.

'So you've come back,' she was saying. 'Did you have a good time in Paris?'

He looked down at her curiously. 'Have you missed me?' he mocked.

Despairingly, Felicity knew he did not regard anything he had done to be questionable, and while it angered her more it also made her feel helpless. She saw him through a mist of tears and closed her eyes as he hauled her in his arms. The world was filled with the subtle flavour of his personality, Sandy whinnied his approval and Curt's mouth was firm and clinging on hers.

Frantically she thought, I've ached for this, yet dreaded and feared the complete domination it brings. Where is all that resistance I built up against it? Her hands became useless things in her defence; instead of pushing him away they were as treacherous as her heart, clinging in a shameless disregard for pride. Felicity was flushed and breathless when he let her go, still bemused and giddy with the reaction of his nearness.

Shaken, she looked up, and the mocking light in his eyes acclaiming his arrogant conquest refreshed her memory. The trip to Paris, his masculine assumption that he could do what he liked regardless of her feelings fired her resentment anew. She shivered, and at once he was all concern.

His arm was warm and vital around her shoulders. 'You're cold,' he said tenderly, 'I hope you haven't caught a chill. Come on, let's have breakfast. I'm famished.'

'You're eating nothing,' he said roughly, making a good breakfast himself. 'Come on, let me see you eat.' His look was curious. 'The Colonel all right?'

'Yes.'

'Then what is it?' He grinned. 'You've been pining for me?'

The dark blue eyes meeting his were clear and resolute. 'Why didn't you tell me you were going to Paris?' she asked quietly.

The tilt of his eyebrows was very attractive. He looked startled.

'Should I have done?'

Felicity compressed her lips. 'I was expecting you home on Saturday. Henri cooked dinner and you never came.'

He pushed back his empty plate and used his table napkin. 'Sorry about that. But Roger, my clerk, telephoned you, surely?'

'No, he didn't. In any case, what prevented you from telephoning yourself?'

He picked up one of the morning papers which Henri had placed near them on the table and opened it.

'Pressure of work, for one thing,' he answered laconically.

'And for another?'

He lowered the paper and his eyes glinted dangerously. 'Look here, what is this, an inquisition?'

Felicity lifted her chin. 'You didn't telephone me because you knew that I would object to you going to Paris.'

'My dear girl, your objections don't enter into this, since it's in the line of duty that I went to Paris,' he told her calmly.

She got to her feet and walked to the window, presenting him with a slim back. 'You mean it was nothing to do with the Staffordlys?' she said without turning round.

'I meant nothing of the kind. I'm going to take up the case of Nora Staffordly, who has been arrested on a charge of murdering her husband.'

Felicity swung round, her blue eyes wide. 'How terrible for her! I'm sorry, of course, but I don't see why you should be the one to defend her. There are others who could do so.'

Curt had moved behind her and he put his arms around her, drawing her back against him to talk over her head.

'I'm sorry, my sweet, but I'm already committed. Mrs Staffordly is a very old friend, and I'd be a poor sort of a friend if I refused to help her in her hour of need.'

'But you told me only last week that you were up to your ears in work,' she accused him shakenly. 'You were too busy to come home.'

'True,' he agreed, 'but I couldn't do any other where a friend is concerned.'

'But surely there's some way out. It isn't right, Curt. What about our holiday?'

'That will have to wait. I'm sorry, my sweet. It's going to be hard on you, but I'm sure you wouldn't want me to act any differently. I've given my word, and once I've done that nothing nor no one will make the slightest difference to my decision.'

Felicity did not answer, and a feeling of utter despair swept over her. Slowly he turned her round to face him and she looked up searchingly into his face. Then, with her arms winding themselves around his neck, she said pleadingly, 'Please, Curt, let someone else take the case. Please. . . .'

'Darling,' he said, and there was a firmness in his voice which told her the answer even before he said it, 'I will not have you interfering in my work. The answer is no, a very definite no. The time will soon go, and afterwards I shall make plans to take Roger into a partnership with me. Judge Greatman wants me to follow in his footsteps, and I've promised him that I'll think about it again when he's due to retire. It will give me more home life if I accept.'

She stared at him pitifully, and was silent. There was nothing to say, nothing to do but accept his decision. What power she had over him was as strong as he would let it be, and no more. No doubt he loved her and needed her love in return, but he would not be swayed by it in any way.

That Sunday and the Monday, Curt was with her and not with her. Attentive and teasing as he was, he gave the impression that his thoughts were elsewhere; yet she could not complain, since he was everything a woman needed from a man, a perfect lover and a man with whom one felt sheltered and protected. It would have been easier for her had he been thoughtless and cruel—at least then his going would not mean so much. But he was with her all the time he could spare despite his many commitments, coming home each evening and even managing to lunch with her in town until the end of the week and his departure for Paris.

On their last evening at home, Felicity was torn between asking to go with him and staying home. He had not asked her to go in any case, knowing as he did that she did not care for Nora Staffordly. There was no reason why she should not go with him, but the torment of knowing the times he would be with Nora Staffordly would become unbearable. And he had promised to come home every weekend, which meant sharing with him a few days completely divorced from his work. During that time he would be hers completely. He was leaving Henri in charge, and was going to stay in a very excellent club in Paris for the time he was to be there.

Felicity had been surprised that he had not made arrangements to stay with his mother at her place. While Madame Moreau did not interfere very much with her son and daughter-in-law, her behaviour with Curt was far different than Elvira's had been with Blain. Which was the reason, Felicity thought, that Curt was stronger in character and not weak like Blain.

'I'd feel better,' Curt said as he kissed her goodbye at the airport, 'if you would stay with your father at Norton Towers while I'm away.'

'I'm staying at home,' she answered, blinking back the tears. 'I want you to myself when you come at the weekend.'

Somehow she managed to tear herself from his arms and her hands groped the empty air as she watched him stride to the plane. She saw them shut the doors, saw the propellers turn and heard the drone of the engines as the men removed the blocks. The service and fire vehicles swung away across the tarmac as they tested the engines, then the ground crew stood back. The plane turned from its stand, entered the runway to run into a final turn before soaring up into the blue, and suddenly it was gone.

CHAPTER ELEVEN

THE first week Curt was away was the longest Felicity had ever lived through. They had been parted so much since their marriage, and she could have borne it more easily had they been married a year or more, when their life together had become more stabilized. He had left her at a time when she was still enchanted with a union of twin souls, her own and his. Her whole world centred upon him. She knew that love to a man was not the same as to a woman—whereas all her waking thoughts were his, Curt's would be filled with his work. His love for her was the softening quality he needed to make him more tender, more human, but it was to him a thing apart. It would never be his whole life.

The first evening on her own she went to dine with her father, and his company did much to bolster her morale. Driving back to Cherry Trees she decided to revert to her old life of entertaining and visiting friends; her father had a dinner party lined up for later in the week and she would fill her days with activities. If the thought of Blain and her mother stung her—as it often did since she found their loss much harder to bear as the days went by—then she would put on a brave front and be thankful for beautiful memories.

Curt came home at the weekend and she flung herself into his arms at the airport. There was nothing of the pale, wan grass widow about her, when she shone up at him with clear, dark blue shining eyes. Her senses were drowned in a sudden rush of joy as the tall figure that spelt magic for her strode to meet her.

'What a welcome!' he exclaimed. Then his mouth was on her eager one, sweet and close.

During those two heavenly days there was no mention of

the Staffordly case. Curt had never talked shop with her, and Felicity had no desire to waste a moment of their time together on subjects she would rather forget.

On Saturday evening he took her to a show in London and they had supper afterwards. Coming back in the car, he said, 'Mother was surprised that I hadn't taken you with me to Paris. I told her it wouldn't be much fun for you, since I would be tied up for the Lord knows how many hours each day, with my work here to contend with too. She did press me to ask you to come back with me, if only for a week or so.'

Had he seconded the invitation, Felicity would have had to have gone back with him; she would not have been able to have helped herself. She was already dreading their parting at the airport the following night. But he said no more and gave his attention to his driving, leaving her painfully conscious of his disturbing presence, his clean-cut look, his air of distinction, his slow quizzical smile that did crazy things to her heart as it sparkled in his eyes before his lips curved.

His return told her only too clearly that this tremendous, incredible feeling she had for him was as strong as ever, and she forced herself to speak because she was afraid of his silence.

'Your mother is a dear,' she said. 'You must thank her for me, and tell her that Daddy is enjoying my company while you're away.'

Felicity went on to tell him about the dinner party the Colonel had given that week, and mentioned the fact that Judge Greatman had been there and had asked after him. He had also asked jokingly when he was going to be a godfather, but Felicity did not mention this to Curt, although she longed for another child. If there were to be any more children then it would have to be because they both wanted them.

So each weekend came and went like a small oasis in the

161

desert of her loneliness, during which she noticed a subtle change taking place in Curt. Each time he came home he grew more demanding of her, as though he could not bear her to be out of his sight. His kisses were rough, his love-making intense and exhausting. Gone was that gentle approach. It seemed to Felicity in her bewilderment that he was using her body for the outlet of his own tension, built up during the week he was away.

This idea became strengthened in her mind by something David Colston had said one night when she met him at the house of a friend. She had gone there to dinner and a ball afterwards, and after dinner when the dancing had begun David had claimed the first dance. He was the perfect dancing partner, and their steps matched perfectly.

'I've missed you,' he said, gliding off with her with a rhythm and sense of timing that made him a joy to partner. 'I was in Paris last week. Thought I'd see you there, since your husband seemed to be always about. How come you aren't with him?'

She said lightly, 'He comes home at weekends, so I keep Daddy company mostly during the week. Curt is very busy with his work, and it wouldn't be much fun mooching around all day waiting for him to come home.'

He let this pass. 'I suppose you know the trial comes up soon. He is defending Mrs Staffordly, isn't he?'

'Yes. That's why he's in Paris.'

'He's got a fight on his hands. You probably know that.'

Felicity missed a step. 'No . . . I didn't. Do you mean . . . the case will go against Mrs Staffordly?'

'I would say,' said David firmly, 'that Mrs Staffordly is going to need all the luck in the world not to be convicted.'

Felicity remembered this as the date for the trial of Nora Staffordly drew closer. Curt came home at weekends taut and glittering, as if she was there solely to please him. Felicity, knowing he was going through a difficult phase, bore with his possessiveness and insatiable demands, and in

162

doing so became more dependent upon him than ever. She began to live only for the weekends when he would be with her. He became like a powerful drug which she craved and could not do without. As the week went by she could not think of him without a tempest of longing drowning her appetite and strength of will. As his needs became more primitive, she lived only to give him pleasure—it mattered little to her that he could do as he wished with her. She only knew that he had the magician's touch that could whip her blood aflame.

Each Friday Felicity was there at the airport, holding her breath until Curt's plane came in and he emerged, virile and darkly intense, holding her gaze with a look that made her pulses race. The brown hands encircling her waist were as hard and compelling as his mouth as it closed over hers. Such moments were to be recalled later when he had gone; on her sleepless pillow she was to turn wretchedly in search of sleep, in a vain attempt to forget her bodily hunger for him.

Then one Friday he did not arrive; he sent a telegram to say he had been delayed. The next morning it was in all the newspapers.

Nora Staffordly found not guilty. Brilliant defence counsel saves life of beautiful socialite.

A month went by, during which time Felicity suffered like one bereaved. She waited in vain for Curt to come, longing for the strength of his arms, his kisses and the thud of his heart against her own. She told no one of her misery and fear that she had lost him; perhaps he had never been hers to lose. Pride kept her from writing or telephoning him. Now the hunting season had started again the Colonel was riding to hounds, and filling his days pleasurably; it had made her feel much better to see him take an interest in things again, and she had waved him off gladly when he had gone to spend a week or so with an old friend in Sussex. He had been away a week when Curt came home.

Felicity was in the garden when the sound of his car broke the silence. From her vantage point behind the rose bushes she watched him stride into the house, then calmly put down her flower basket and, dropping her gardening gloves inside it, followed him in. Henri was taking his time going thoughtfully through the hall to the kitchen when she entered. His glance at her was curious, but he smiled and glanced sideways to the staircase. She smiled back and was not sure whether his penetrating eye had seen her sudden withdrawn tenseness.

'Hello, my sweet. The prodigal has returned.'

Curt had strode lightly to the rail at the head of the stairs on not finding her, and was leaning on it smiling down at her. Felicity studied, with senses sharpened by pain, the elegant pose of his lean body as he leaned against the rail. His kinetic magnetism and charm, the air of self-assurance radiating from him, was as disturbing as ever, and it was not until that moment that she realized how her tense anxiety had dulled her emotions. She was perfectly calm.

'Hello,' she replied, walking gracefully up the stairs towards him, her slender hand gripping the rail in order to steady it. 'Congratulations! So you won the case. Mrs Staffordly will be pleased.'

'Pleased?' he echoed. 'Come now, that's rather mild coming from you and, come to think of it, so is the welcome. Come here.'

He gripped her shoulders, drew her towards him and kissed her. A firm hard kiss. Her own lips were skilfully casual and he let her go, the few lines time had etched in his forehead deepening as he frowned down at her.

'You look thinner. Have you been eating?'

Eating? Felicity could have laughed had the situation not been so tragic. How could one eat when the ache for human contact made one feel physically sick? He wouldn't understand that. He would never understand a woman's feelings. He slid an arm around her shoulders and placed his finger under her chin. Her heart lurched as he claimed her lips and the sudden pounding of it made her panic and go tense.

But she hid her feelings well. One didn't go through a scene hundreds of times a day like reading from a script without becoming word-perfect.

She drew away from him gently, and even managed to smile up at him.

'How long are you staying?' she asked evenly as they strolled into their room.

'Eh? Just a minute, I've only just arrived, Mrs Moreau.'

He was studying her with a maddening expression on his face, and his voice vibrated deep down inside her like a gong.

'So you have. On another weekend flight, I presume.'

He darkened beneath his tan and moved as though to take her in his arms. With her blue eyes flashing, her face beautifully flushed, she was lovely and very desirable. But he was not going to let her catechise him. He was his own master and was not going to be dictated to by any woman.

Coolly, he said, 'As a matter of fact, it is. I have to go back to tie up a few loose ends before moving office back to London. Don't look so cross, my sweet.'

He pulled her to him, kissing her with demanding force. But Felicity did not yield an inch. Her legs were becoming weak and her resolve was ebbing away, but if she did not tell him now the matter would drag on and she had already had more than she could bear. And she meant it so sincerely that it was quite an effort to stem the tears. So she told herself fiercely to keep her emotions in check, and met the hard glint in his eyes as he released her, gently but with a firm resolve.

He was puzzled, she could tell, as he asked quietly, 'What's happened? I come home on the crest of a wave because I've won my case and everything is going so well. My sweet, I don't understand.'

'Was that why you haven't been home all these weeks? Is

it the reason that you're now on the crest of a wave, as you put it, because Nora Staffordly is free?'

'Naturally.' His frown deepened. 'Oh, come, my sweet, I know you haven't much time for Nora, but you did want me to win my case and set her free.' He laughed, turning her round to face him when she would have turned away, and looked down into her passionate face. Slow shock drenched her from head to toe at his admission that his happiness stemmed purely from Nora Staffordly and not from coming home to his wife. Reckless, tearing anger was behind her strength as she thrust him from her.

'How dare you come home to me admitting your . . . your involvement with that woman! You insult me by ignoring my existence for six weeks, and insult me further by daring to say that I hated Nora Staffordly enough to wish for her conviction. I hate you! I never want to see you again. Go back to your fancy woman—you deserve each other. I don't want you!' she cried angrily, and ran into his adjoining dressing room to slam the door and lock it in his face.

How long she stayed there Felicity was never quite certain. She didn't cry. She was beyond tears as she lay across the divan, her face hidden in her arms. Curt had hammered peremptorily just twice on the door, then everything was silent.

'Felicity, open this door or I shall break it down. Do you hear?' he had threatened furiously. It had been a threat and no more. Behind the closed door there was complete silence. Dry sobs came from inside the depths of her being, relieving the nervous tension which for weeks had been pushing her closer to an emotional abyss. And gradually she became calm.

Curt was waiting for her in their bedroom when she finally opened the communicating door to stand in the aperture. Uncurling his long length from a chair near the door, he rose to his feet to confront her.

His face was an enigmatic mask through which no gleam

came. In desperation, Felicity lifted an appealing look in an effort to get through his defences, to try to convey to him a little of what she had suffered, was still suffering. But there was no softening in him, and there was no escape. She might have been facing him in court.

'I think I'm entitled to an explanation of your conduct,' he said coldly.

He loomed before her, larger than life, his eyes as hard as steel. She was seeing him again in the splendour of his robes as they accentuated his hard, perfectly built body, the deadly keenness of his eyes and the arrogant look of a man who had carved out a brilliant career for himself without the help of a woman. But he had taken her and made her his, then put her away in a filing cabinet like one of his discarded briefs, to be taken out, looked at and fondled as it pleased him. And like everything else he had set his mind to, he had made her his for all time and spoiled her for any other man. Even now, while she hated his arrogance and cold, peremptory demand, there was something sweet and untouched about her that he had revered on the first night of their marriage and which, she knew, would always respond to him.

Wearily, she said, 'An explanation, if any, surely should come from you—or don't I count in your life any more?'

'I've nothing to explain,' he replied forcefully. 'I've defended Mrs Staffordly as I always do any other clients, to the best of my ability. It hasn't made the slightest difference to our relationship. I have simply been her defence counsel.'

She quivered and clenched her hands. 'And do your clients always come before your wife?'

Curt drew in his breath raspingly. 'So you're jealous. You've seen my association with Nora Staffordly as some clandestine affair which you wrongly imagine has been going on for years. You're being absurd, maligning a woman whom you know nothing about. She has been unfortunate, that's all.'

Felicity's chin tilted militantly. 'How right you are! I only know that she's been unfortunate for me. First Blain, then. . . .' she stopped suddenly and drew a deep breath. 'I beg your pardon. I should have said first you, then Blain, in that order.'

A muscle tightened in his cheek and his eyes glinted dangerously. Holding her breath, Felicity watched him beat back the anger in his eyes until there was nothing there but a sudden weariness, and she ached longingly to smooth the look from his face.

'I can see I'm wasting my time talking to you in this mood. Who's changed you? David Colston?' he demanded.

'That's right, put the blame on David,' she cried. 'At least he wouldn't have left me so soon for another woman.'

He waved a contemptuous hand. 'He hasn't got the wit to take a wife, much less leave her for another woman.'

'He proposed to me often enough. I wish now that I'd accepted him,' she retorted.

There followed a deadly silence and he looked down at her grimly.

'Maybe it isn't too late,' he said, and turning on his heel, left her.

Felicity went home to Norton Towers that night, packing a suitcase and driving over in her car. She did not see Curt again. The next morning she went back to Cherry Trees for more of her things, telling Henri that he must take his orders now from Curt, as she would not be coming back.

Sandy, her horse, was installed once again in his old stable and he whinnied with delight to be back again among his old friends. Felicity smiled wryly, glad that at least someone was not unhappy about the move.

Anna was dumbstruck. 'You must be barmy to leave that dishy man,' she said, 'you'll never get another half as exciting.'

168

'Who wants another?' Felicity said crossly. 'One is enough for me. You can keep your men.'

And she meant it. Any woman who let herself care too deeply for any man deserved what was coming to her, she told herself in a misery of unhappiness.

'Don't mention Curt's name to me again, Anna. I don't want to hear anything about him,' she said dully.

And Anna, looking at her aghast, saw something more shattering than grief in the pale, steady composure of her face.

She protested, 'But he's sure to get in touch with you. What shall I tell him?'

Felicity shook her head wearily. 'Nothing. He won't bother to get in touch. He has his pride, besides. . . .' She paused, remembering his face when she had confessed her regret at not marrying David Colston. She had not meant that; the words had rushed out in the heat of anger to act as a balm to her pride, a pride that rises up in every woman when her husband turns to another woman. It was better that Anna should not know this, for Felicity knew that Anna's deep regard for her would not hesitate in trying to heal the breach between herself and Curt.

In the weeks that passed Norton Towers was to her a refuge, a place of peace and comfort with the rest of the world shut out. Gradually the numb feeling around her heart melted and she began to take notice, to savour again little pleasures from the familiar things she loved. Cherry Trees had been shut up and Henri had moved back to be with Curt. Curt had made two appointments with her, but she had taken care to be out when he had called.

They had been arranged through Anna, since she herself had refused to answer the telephone. The second time he had come, Felicity had fled into the woods nearby until he had gone. She had heard his car draw up with a wildly beating heart, and his presence had been like a magnet drawing her to the house. Her agonizing need of him struck

169

her to the heart like a mortal blow from a dagger. Her whole being cried out for him; it always would, for theirs was no ordinary love, the bonds that bound them together were like a blood relationship which on her part could never die.

In that hour of agony, while she waited for him to leave, she lay on the sweet-smelling grass beneath the friendly shelter of trees, as still as death and crushed by the overwhelming sense of loss. The shadows had lengthened into evening when, with no more tears to shed, Felicity stumbled back to the house, avoiding Anna as she went to her room.

CHAPTER TWELVE

A FEW weeks after her quarrel and subsequent parting from Curt, Felicity received a visit from his mother. She had written previously expressing her regret and pain at their parting, which she refused to believe was final.

After a brief silence she arrived. Felicity greeted her warmly, more in the light of a friend than as her mother-in-law; nor did she herself feel like the younger Mrs Moreau, exactly. One of the most unsettling things about her visit was that Felicity knew why she had come. As usual she looked very chic, with a pearly glow to her creamy skin and a hint of green eye-shadow. The model two-piece suit she wore, in lilac with a gay little hat and matching tasselled scarf, was enchanting. Her whole aura was soft, sweet and coaxing.

Anna brought in afternoon tea and they were alone; the Colonel was out at a Parish Council meeting. Madame Moreau came straight to the point as she graciously accepted a cup of tea.

Holding it daintily, she said, 'I was surprised when you didn't come to Paris with Curt. I've no wish to pry, but I can't help but wonder whether it had any bearing on this break between you.'

Felicity picked up her own cup and saucer. Her voice seemed to come from a distance, thick and tremulous.

'It began long before that. I'm referring to Curt's association with Nora Staffordly.'

'Ah! So that was it.'

Felicity's heart beat painfully. Her tea tasted like dust and ashes in her mouth. As yet she had not composed herself, and would have preferred more notice of Madame Moreau's impending visit, but as it was she sat before her guest like someone prepared for a recriminatory trial. Her parting from Curt was too recent to be anything but painful, and it was all like a bad dream.

She said bitterly, 'Surely you knew? People gossip, and Nora Staffordly is one of their favourite topics of conversation.'

With hands not quite steady Felicity put down her cup and saucer to the low table nearby, noting that her words had gone home.

'I'm sorry,' Madame Moreau began, it seemed, with an effort, 'I should have told you before, but somehow I couldn't. Not after you told me about your brother Blain being spoiled by his mother. I can't even begin to explain why I was so smug in allowing you to believe what a sensible mother I'd been, when it wasn't like that at all.'

Madame Moreau put down her cup and used a wisp of lace to touch her lips delicately.

'I'll try to explain,' she continued with a sad smile. 'I've had two sons. Raoul, my firstborn, was a premature baby and not strong. He was a pretty baby and I lavished all my love and care upon him; he was four and dreadfully spoilt when Curt was born. Curt was strong and self-sufficient from a very early age. I was too wrapped up in Raoul to give him much attention, so he became his father's boy from the beginning.

'Nora Staffordly was Nora Leigh then. She was a neighbour of ours, and the children grew up together. Although Curt was the youngest, he was more mature than Raoul, and also he hadn't much time for girls. He was very fond of his father, but he did encourage Raoul's friendship with Nora. He was the first to congratulate them on their engagement, and his father was pleased, seeing in Nora a steadying influence for Raoul, who could never hold a job down for any length of time after university. After his engagement Raoul took an advertising job, and seemed to be settling down.'

Her voice trembled to a close and she reached for her tea to drink the rest of it before continuing.

'Raoul was killed on the night before the wedding. He was returning home from a bachelor party when his car ran into a wall.' A wisp of lace was raised to her nose and eyes. 'He left Nora expecting his baby. Curt offered to marry her for the child's sake, but it seemed that Nora had had more than enough of the Moreaus. She refused and married Clifford Staffordly instead. It happened when my husband was falsely accused of embezzlement; the baby died soon after it was born, and Nora changed overnight to become a good-time girl. Her marriage to Clifford Staffordly was unhappy from the start, and Curt never ceased to feel responsible for her unhappiness.'

Quiveringly aware that the conversation was as painful to Madame Moreau as it was to her, Felicity said gently, 'Thank you for telling me this. It can't have been easy for you.' She leaned forward and patted her hand in sympathy. 'How terrible for you to lose your husband and son in such tragic circumstances! However, you must see that what you've told me doesn't alter things between Curt and me. In fact it only strengthens my belief that Curt is and has always been in love with Nora Staffordly.'

Madame's shrug was typically French, and it occurred to Felicity that her journey had been made more from a sense of duty than love for Curt. Felicity began to understand why his mother had never intruded much in their marriage; her heart was buried with Raoul, her favourite son. It was a case of Elvira and Blain over again. Poor Curt! But he did not need her sympathy, he was self-sufficient. She was relieved when her visitor refused to prolong her call, on the excuse that she planned to do some shopping in London before returning home.

Maybe it was the haunting sadness in the alluring blue eyes, veiled with dark curling lashes much longer than her own, that made Madame Moreau take the hand of the girl she had become so fond of to make a last appeal.

'I'm sure you're wrong about Curt and Nora. He feels a sense of duty towards her, nothing more,' she stated firmly.

'I wish I could believe you,' answered Felicity.

That evening at dinner, she had two things to tell her father; the first was about Madame Moreau's visit.

'So she came to patch things up between you and Curt,' he said when she had finished. His eyebrows raised hopefully. 'Did she succeed?'

'No, Daddy,' she answered emphatically.

He frowned. 'I know this isn't my affair,' he said quietly, 'I don't intend to interfere, but you've married a fine man, my dear.' His voice trembled with feeling. 'And whatever your attitude, you owe it to him to give him a fair hearing.'

Felicity went white and gazed at him with a set face. 'I can't, Daddy. Something has happened. I will not have Curt returning to me from a sense of duty because I'm expecting another child.'

The Colonel was almost overcome by the news that he was to become a grandfather. His voice trembled with emotion.

'My poor child,' he said, 'I can't help but be thrilled at the thought of having a companion in my old age. At the same time you must see that Curt, as the baby's father, has a right to know.'

Felicity shook her head. 'I don't want him to know.' Her voice was clear and decisive, her blue eyes were pleading. 'Promise me you won't tell him.'

The Colonel's voice was tender. 'It's entirely up to you, of course, but he'll be sure to hear about it sooner or later.'

Felicity paused for a moment. 'Since I've decided to have the baby here at Norton Towers, Curt won't know about it until after it's born—not even then, with luck. He could decide to settle down in Paris by then.' She swallowed on the roughness in her throat. 'His interests lie in that direction.'

The Colonel shook his head, and reluctantly agreed.

In the days and weeks that followed, Felicity ran through a whole gamut of emotions. The empty void Curt had left in her daily life smarted like an open wound; she not only knew the loneliness of the body but also the loneliness of the spirit when her senses were dulled to everything around her. Then gradually the baby she had so bitterly resented now became a lifeline. He would be hers, and loneliness when he arrived would be no more.

Most of her time was spent outdoors and she went for long walks, rising early in the morning in order to tire herself out for a good night's sleep. Since it was now summer again, most of her friends were away on holiday; David Colston had gone with his mother to stay in Malta for six months, so she relied on the beauty of the grounds at Norton Towers to give her a peace and contentment spent mostly in the company of her father. The Colonel was very kind and considerate in her days of waiting, making them less tedious and dreary by walking or sitting with her, playing chess or her favourite records.

News of Curt trickled through from time to time. He was working between London and Paris and once she saw a photograph of him taken at a reception in Paris with Nora Staffordly. It was in one of the monthly magazines, and had been taken at a chateau outside Paris where they were the guests of a duke whose name had become famous through the wines he produced.

Felicity's baby slipped quietly into the world one night, a beautiful boy so like Curt that she wanted to cry. The Colonel was delighted, and Anna glowed with pride.

'He's a real Curt Moreau,' she cried, holding the baby in her arms. 'He always will be, no matter what you call him.'

Motherhood suited Felicity, giving her the glow of health and a return to her slimness. Her days were now filled with the baby, and her nights too. She insisted on looking after him herself, lying awake long after she had fed him in the night, thinking of Curt and still finding the ache for him unbearable. She had not touched the allowance he sent her monthly, a very generous one, through his solicitors.

The baby was a month old when, one day, Anna came up to the nursery where Felicity was changing the baby to say that she had a visitor.

'He's here,' she announced dramatically.

Felicity felt her heart take a sudden dive. 'Who's here?' she said through pale lips, and put a hand to her heart.

'Your husband,' was the calm reply. 'Shall I tell him you're here?'

'No, no,' Felicity scooped up the baby from her lap and handed him to her, 'I'll go down. Stay here with the baby.'

At the door, her trembling fingers grasping the knob, she said, 'Where's Daddy?'

'I've no idea.' Anna smiled. 'You're not afraid of your own husband, are you?'

Felicity left the room, angry with Anna for being deliberately unhelpful and her father for not being about when he was wanted. It was evident to her overwrought state that she could expect no help from that quarter; she had to face Curt alone. He had come, of course, because he had heard about the baby. No doubt he had seen the announcement in *The Times*.

With her legs feeling like useless props, she went downstairs to the lounge and stood outside the door, wishing fervently for her father to appear. But there was no sound. She needed every ounce of courage to open the door. He was standing gazing through the window with his back to her, and her eyes rested on the outline of his well-shaped head, poised so proudly on wide shoulders. Hungrily, Felicity took every detail of him, loving the perfect grooming that had always been a part of his charm.

Slowly he turned around to face her, and her heart beat in thick heavy strokes.

'Hello, Felicity,' he said, pushing his hands into his pockets and glowering at her. 'I don't know why you're looking at me so big-eyed and frightened—hate me if you wish, but never be afraid of me. I would never hurt a hair of your beautiful head. Won't you sit down?'

He gestured to a chair with a lean brown hand, and she shook her head.

'Why have you come?' she asked, taking care to leave plenty of space between them. He took his time in answering, allowing his eyes to move slowly, deliberately over the lovely contours of her face and neck, the glittering golden hair and the exquisite lines of her slender figure.

He raised an exasperating brow. 'Surely you know? I saw it in the paper. *That's* why I'm here.'

Felicity groped for the nearest chair blindly, and every scrap of colour left her face. She stood grasping the back of it and staring at him dumbly.

'My poor sweet,' Curt strode towards her, 'does he mean so much to you?'

She swallowed, and her voice seemed to come from a long way off.

'He's my life. He's mine and I'll never give him up.'

He was standing above her. His face had changed colour too; the bronze of his tan went sallow and a muscle moved in his cheek. The one dominant thought going through her mind at that moment was that he had not altered at all. And neither had she. Her desire for him ran through her like a sword to her heart, remembering moments of flame, of love and tenderness. He was harder, leaner, his eyes dark and glinting, probing the misery of longing in her own. He was willing her to look at him so that nothing else mattered, except the old relentless magnetism that drew her to him like steel to steel. Was it love or hate, this passion that ran through her tearing her apart?

For a moment the baby was forgotten as Curt's hands gripped her shoulders with bone-cracking intensity. His touch vibrated along her nerves until she was not herself any more. In fact she could swear that for a fleeting second the need in his eyes for her was as agonizing as hers was for him. She had imagined it, of course.

He was looking at her now with murder in his eyes, and only pride prevented her from crying out at the grip of his powerful hands as he shook her.

'Do you know what you've said?' he demanded. 'You're telling your husband that you can't live without another man.'

Felicity stared up at him in bewilderment. 'What other man? I don't understand. What are you talking about?'

His anger was still there, but he talked like a man being tolerant against his will. He had stopped shaking her and his grip had slackened.

'David Colston. Who else? For God's sake, tell me the truth. Is there someone else, someone I don't know about?' His eyes blazed. 'How many men have you had?'

The sound of her hand coming into contact with his cheek was like the crack of a whip in the stillness of the room. Suddenly he let go of her and swung round to walk to the window.

'I'm sorry,' he said in a low voice. 'That was unforgiveable, contemptible too, because I know you aren't like that. I'm afraid I'm not myself today. When I saw the announcement of Colston's engagement in the newspaper I had to come, in case you were upset about it.'

'David engaged? I can't believe it!'

Felicity's voice sounded hoarse with surprise. Then suddenly he heard her laugh, a laugh of such pure pleasure that it swung him round to look at her incredulously.

'Fancy missing that,' she gurgled. 'Is it anyone I know? Do tell me her name. You did say that he hadn't the wit to take a wife.'

'You mean you didn't know?' he demanded.

'Of course I didn't! Is it someone he's met in Malta? I

believe he's there on holiday with his mother. She won't be a bit happy about it, she adores her beloved son.'

Suddenly Felicity was reminded of her own son asleep upstairs, and was aware that Curt knew nothing about him. The smile faded from her face.

He said wearily, 'It's all right, there was no need to put on an act. You must be feeling like hell.'

She was, but not in the way he meant. 'I didn't think it mattered to you how I felt. I'm sure you haven't thought of me at all in the last seven months—why should it suddenly matter to you now?'

'For two reasons,' he told her grimly, 'the first is that you are my wife.' He paused and looked right into her eyes. 'I don't think you'll be interested in the second.'

Felicity said quietly, 'Why not tell me, and then you'll know.'

She was trembling now, alone as she was in the room with him. She was afraid, desperately afraid of him, afraid of something she did not understand except that the present moment was one of the most crucial in her life. She could not look at him for the life of her—but she felt his eyes as he came across the room to where she stood.

The room held a listening quality, as if waiting for the sound of the deep voice that never failed to vibrate inside her.

'I came because I love you,' he told her simply and quietly. 'I couldn't bear to think of what you might be going through because of Colston. You told me that you wished you'd married him instead of me—what further proof could I have that you didn't love me any more?'

Felicity drowned in the exquisite silence enfolding them. She spoke through lips softly parted, her voice so low that he had to bend his head to hear it.

'You did say that you loved me. Please say it again. Please,' she entreated, raising her head to see the look in his eyes that already answered her in no uncertain terms.

179

'I love you with every drop of blood that's in me,' he said very gently, as his arms closed around her. 'I've never wanted any other woman in my life as I've wanted you. I never shall.'

He bent his head, and his breath was warm on her lips. The look in his eyes made her tremble and she tried to speak, but no sound came. Gradually her arms crept up to frame his face with her hands as she gave him her lips. For a long time Felicity drowned in the bliss of his arms as time stood still. She was carried along on a wave of passion; his kisses burned her lips, his arms squeezed the breath from her body, and she had to cling on to the powerful curve of his shoulder blades. But her passion was equal to his as his kisses whipped up the answering flames within her. It was not until she eventually held him off, palpitating and exhausted with her hands against his chest, that sanity returned.

The light of masculine triumph in his eyes brought her back to banalities.

'But how can you say you love me?' she cried. 'You've left me alone for seven months without a word.'

'After I called to see you when you'd taken care to be out,' he answered grimly. 'And don't forget that you implied that you loved Colston.'

'What if I'd put in for a divorce? Would you have given me one?'

'No, by heaven, I wouldn't. I'd have come quick enough at the first sign of a petition. You're my wife, and you're going to stay that way.' His hands bit into her shoulders again. 'I have to go away again to finish something important; then I shall be back, and to stay. Do you understand?'

Felicity stared up at him unbelievingly. 'You ... you're going now? You've only just come! After seven months you coolly walk in here and take your leave again like ... like someone selling something, who'll be round again in seven months' time. How dare you?' Reckless, searing anger gave her strength. All the scorn she was capable of rose in her voice.

'All right,' she cried passionately, 'go back to Nora Staffordly, but I don't want you. Don't ever come back!' She hated him from the arrogant poise of his head to the tips of his well-shod feet. Tears blinded her eyes as he silenced her in the only way.

His mouth smothered the protests on her lips and gradually she went quiet against him. Again Felicity felt the quick leap of her pulses. It was no use fighting him. They were two incomplete halves until they came together. Were he to go away now—were she to refuse to see him again—it would make no difference. They would belong to each other until the end of their lives, together or apart.

'My foolish darling,' he whispered as his lips caressed her face, 'I'm not going back to Nora Staffordly I've been working as technical adviser to the French courts. Another week or so will suffice for me to finish what I set out to do, and then I shall be home for good.' He consulted his watch. 'I have to go.' Suddenly he was smiling down at her, tenderly, boyishly. 'I had it all worked out; I had to come back to London for an important conference and I stole time off to come here and carry you back with me, whether you wanted to go or not. I wish I had known how you really felt about David Colston before—I wouldn't have taken on this work if I had, and given you, as I thought, time to make up your mind about where you and I stood. Will you come back with me?'

His voice held a caress that drew her very soul from her body, reminding her of the small son upstairs who would grow up just as charming and vital as his father. It was on the tip of her tongue to tell him about his son, but there was no time. It would only divert Curt from the work he had in hand. Besides, she wanted to see the look dawn slowly in his eyes when she placed his son in his arms, the look of a proud father. Later, she wanted that look replaced by that of a lover, and to know the bliss of a reunion in his arms.

So she said, 'I want to wait here for you.' The blue eyes raised to his were filled with her love for him. 'I love you so much that I want all of you, not just the part that your work has spared to me. Do you mind so much if I do that?'

Infinite tenderness was in his smile, and something humble that was not at all like Curt Moreau. Gently he took her hands in his warm clasp and kissed them, knowing that she enriched his life with her melting warmth and tenderness. Their separation had taught him much, learned though he was in material things. He had known that when he really fell in love he would fall harder than most; what he had not known was that he was one of those chosen few who would have a woman fashioned for him alone, the one woman who could make his blood leap and his heart quicken its rhythm.

'You want me to come here to you at Norton Towers?' he said.

Felicity nodded. 'Yes. You'll know why when you come.'

'Shall I, my sweet?' He gave a painful smile. 'The next week or so are going to be the longest I've ever lived through.'

Ten days later Curt's plane touched down at the airport, and he drove to Norton Towers well above the speed limit. The car lanes were filled with impatient drivers like himself, and a tender smile curved his well-cut lips. The gates of the drive were open and he sped along it, braked and was out of the car in seconds. The house slumbered in the sunshine and there seemed to be no one about, but the front door was open. Anna met him in the hall to answer the unspoken query in his eyes.

'The second door to the right at the head of the stairs,' she told him, with a twinkle in her eyes.

He took the stairs two at a time, knocked and opened the door. The room he entered was filled with sunlight, spilling through snow white, nylon frilled curtains. But it was not the fact that it was a nursery that caused Curt to go pale; it was the sight of Felicity, bending over a cot to lift out a small bundle in her arms. A constriction arose in his throat as, silent and intent, his brain registered a picture he would cherish all his life.

She was wearing a button-through blue linen dress and white sandals, and his eyes were on the beautiful line of her neck, on the delicate profile of her small head with the shining golden hair and the exquisite, minute details of her appearance that never failed to please his fastidious eye. She was looking down at the small bundle in her arms as if even now she could not believe it was there. He held his breath as she looked up, and suddenly laughing blue eyes met his over the bundle in her arms.

'Curt,' she cried, 'come and say hello to your son. Isn't he beautiful?'

Words failed Curt as he reached her side and tentatively took the baby in his arms. He looked down on a tuft of hair and a tiny face so like his own that he had to grin.

'He's wonderful,' he said. 'Why didn't you tell me?'

'I have,' she answered, 'in the nicest possible way. You won't be so lucky over the next—you'll have to go through all the agonies of being an expectant father.'

She smiled up at him, and the look in his eyes made her lower her own.

Darkly, he said, 'Wait until I put our son and heir down, my girl. I'll show you that I'm a force to be reckoned with.' And he did. His embrace was enchanting, his face still cool from outdoors, his lips warm and urgent. He kissed her as if he would never let her go, and her hands moved blindly over his head, caressing it. She was where she belonged; the magic of her old life had gone. There was no magic for her now except in her husband's arms.

He kissed her eyelids, the tip of her nose and the warm hollow of her throat.

Against her hair, he murmured, 'I ought to beat you for holding out on me, but I'll forgive you since you've given me such a wonderful present. I have one for you too, not counting myself, of course.'

He laughed down at her, and Felicity looked up at him severely.

'You're still arrogant, and far too sure of yourself. I must be mad to saddle myself another one exactly like you.'

He gave her a mocking, tender appraisal. 'You're deliciously mad, my sweet. And very, very beautiful. Motherhood suits you. You don't know what a relief it is to me to know that when I put you in the family way again.'

He laughed silently into her hair at her shocked look, and she felt the chuckle of his happiness vibrating against her. Then he sobered.

'Do you know what I want more than anything else in the world?' he whispered. 'I want to be with you for all time, waking and sleeping, making love to you, sharing your children, your laughter and your life. But first I want to know why you turned against me and let me believe that you wished you'd married David Colston. I know I neglected you during the time I was in Paris, but believe me, it was to my own cost. It was during that parting that I realized how much you meant to me. When my father died I became a dedicated man to his cause; I studied for the bar and nothing else mattered to me except my career after I'd cleared his name.

'Then I met you, and everything was changed overnight. You brought love and tenderness into my life and made me a complete being when before I was just an automaton. I'll never forget how shattered I was when you told me about Colston.' He gave a short, harsh laugh. 'I could have strangled him with my bare hands! I felt the same when I read of his engagement to someone else—I wanted to hurt him as I thought he had hurt you.'

And because he was looking down at her so tenderly,

Felicity told him about Nora Staffordly.

'I've been awfully jealous, darling,' she confessed. 'I honestly thought there was something between you that had begun long before I met you.'

'You still do, don't you?' he demanded, looking down into her eyes searchingly.

She hesitated, but only for a second. 'No. No, I don't,' she answered, and decided she did not care. She thought, some day he will tell me. I shall never ask him. If there's something he doesn't want me to know, so be it. I love him and I have him with me, nothing else matters.

He evidently found her reply convincing, for he smiled and placed an arm around her shoulders.

'Shall we go in search of my suitcase? I put the packet in there.'

They strolled quietly from the nursery and along the corridor to her bedroom, where they found his suitcase. Opening it, he took out a neat, flat parcel which he handed to her.

'For you, my sweet,' he said.

Felicity opened it to see a white, leather-bound book, gold-edged and with the words, 'Our Baby' written in gold on the cover. Her glance at Curt told her he was as surprised as she was to see it. He came and looked over her shoulder as she flicked open the pages gaily designed for details of the baby's birth and christening; further on there were spaces for photographs of the baby's progress.

In between the pages was a letter addressed to Felicity.

It began, 'Thank you for lending me your husband in my greatest hour of need. I want you to have this book for your baby when you have one. It was originally intended for mine, but I lost the baby and the father too. When you receive this I shall be with the man I love, as you will be. I would like you to know that Curt was desperately unhappy all the time he was away from you; please forgive me for any distress I have caused you and your family. I was very

185

fond of Blain, but Raoul was the only man I ever loved. Be happy. Nora Staffordly.'

Felicity, reading the last few lines through a blur of tears, felt Curt take the book and letter from her gently. Then he gathered her to him and said quietly, 'Nora died two days ago in Switzerland. The book came this morning to my club in Paris.'

'Oh, Curt!' she cried, and crumpled against him.

Between them they bathed the baby and put him to bed, all rosy and replete with his feed, then they had dinner with the Colonel. He was delighted to know that they were going to stay with him for a while, and seemed to shed years. As for Curt, his amazing vitality was more dominant than ever, and Felicity was as beautiful as only a happy woman could be. But she seemed to Curt, watching her with a lover's anxious eye, to be rather wistful when she thought no one was noticing.

It was much later, when they were about to retire, that Curt suggested to her that they should take a short stroll in the grounds before bed. A faint breeze stirred the trees, wafting the perfume of the grounds towards them. The scent of the roses was all around them as they reached a seat in a small arbour, and Curt pushed her down into it gently before lowering himself beside her.

'I don't want you to accept Nora's gift,' he told her, 'I should hate to think it makes you unhappy.'

'Oh, but, Curt, it doesn't! I love it so much that I want to cry,' Felicity hastened to assure him.

'Exactly,' he cut in. 'Let's talk about it, shall we?'

Drawing her close against him, he began.

'I never told you about my brother Raoul. I would have got around to it some day, I suppose, but it's important that I tell you now. He was always very close to my mother, which was understandable seeing that he was four years old when I was born, but consequently he was spoiled from birth. He was quite likeable, and I was fond of him, and when he died somehow Nora, being his fiancée, became my responsibility. So I proposed to her for the sake of the child. She refused me and married Staffordly. She could have been moderately happy with him had he been an understanding man, but he wasn't; he couldn't stand the thought of her still being in love with Raoul, although she had married him. After the baby died there were rows, and she finally sought the company of other men.

'I'm sure she saw much in your brother Blain that reminded her of Raoul. All her young men friends were the same type—it seemed that she was searching for his image in someone else. Just before her husband was found dead her doctor had told her that she was suffering from cancer. She kept it to herself and told no one. In a panic at the thought of the pain she would suffer towards the end, she dissolved tablets that were deadly when taken with alcohol, but she put the glass down to answer the telephone. When she came back to the room her husband had picked the drink up and swallowed it. He had been drinking heavily at his club, and he was pretty well under the influence of drink when he arrived home.'

'How terrible! What a tragedy,' Felicity said on a shudder, and he drew her closer.

He agreed. 'It is, especially as they discovered during the post-mortem on Clifford Staffordly that he hadn't long to live in any case. His liver was in a bad state through his excessive drinking. I only saw Nora once after the trial, and that was at the château of a mutual friend. She kept her illness from me and spent the last few months of her life in a clinic in Switzerland; the solicitor acting on her behalf told me this in a letter he sent with the present for you.'

'I shall treasure that present all my life, and when we put the photographs of our baby in it I shall imagine her looking over our shoulders and smiling happily,' Felicity said. While she felt sorry for the Staffordlys and for Nora in

187

particular, she also knew a feeling of relief. Everything made sense again, and the world was safe and filled with promise. Curt had never been Nora's.

They sat for a long time talking of the future.

'About Cherry Trees,' Curt said at last. 'Do we move back there? I left word for Henri to follow me here.' He tilted her head back gently with hands that were strong and tender and looked down into her eyes. 'It's for you to decide, my sweet. It will be a wrench for the Colonel to part with you now that he's had you here again.'

She shone up at him. 'Darling Curt,' she cried. 'I feel that way too. Would you mind awfully if we stayed on here? After all, the place will be ours some day, and he's so lonely.'

Her blue eyes were very appealing.

Curt smiled and agreed, bringing down his cheek to rest against her hair. Held warm and close in his arms, Felicity tried to take it all in. Moisture gathered on her eyelashes; sitting there in the garden of her lovely old home she had everything she had ever wanted from life, a husband whom she adored and a delicious little son. Her father would never be lonely again.

Gratitude stole sweetly over her as she moved her head to look up at Curt, loving every line of his lean face, his masculine nose and deep, disturbing eyes. The happiness and need in them was for her. She had put it there. She lifted a hand to touch the curve of his cheek, and gave a start at the sound of a rustle in a nearby tree.

Her breath caught and she exclaimed, 'What was that?'

He whispered in her ear, 'Could be a little bird thinking it's time we were in bed.'

He bent his head and his lips met hers in a long, hard kiss.

'Come on, let's go,' he said.

Have you missed any of these best-selling Harlequin Romances?

By popular demand... to help complete your collection of Harlequin Romances

50 titles listed on the following pages...

Harlequin Reissues

Harlequin Reissues

Complete and mail this coupon today!